Desert Roots

The Wolves of Twin Moon Ranch
Book 6

by Anna Lowe

Twin Moon Press

Contents

visit www.annalowebooks.com

Free Books

Get your free e-books now!

Sign up for my newsletter at *annalowebooks.com* to get three free books!

- *Desert Wolf*: Friend or Foe (Book 1.1 in the Twin Moon Ranch series)

- *Off the Charts* (the prequel to the Serendipity Adventure series)

- *Perfection* (the prequel to the Blue Moon Saloon series)

Chapter One

Luke tightened his grip on the worn steering wheel of his pickup. Damn, did he miss his Ducati. The wind in his hair. Asphalt rolling under the wheels. The 750cc motor humming with a life of its own. That feeling of utter freedom that always filled him on cool desert nights like this, when a thousand stars dotted the sky and an open landscape stretched to infinity on both sides of the road. The kind of night he would head out on just for the joy of it. No destination. No obligations. No plans.

He gnashed his teeth, spat out the window, and caught a glance of his own reflection in the mirror. Damn. Even if he were on his bike, he wouldn't have felt the wind in his hair because he'd had it cut short. Straight. Neat. Where the hell had he gotten the idea that a respectable haircut might help him take the first step toward becoming a respectable man?

Who are you trying to kid? a dark voice growled from the back of his mind.

No amount of cleaning up would scrub away the dirty color of his tan or the ink of his tattoos. And no amount of pretending would cleanse away the past.

He took a deep breath and forced his eyes back to the road. This was about looking forward, not back. About a new beginning. And damn it, he'd see this through, no matter what.

A speed limit sign flashed by, and it felt weird, not breaking seventy-five. Not even trying to.

Go a little faster. Chase that high, the dark voice said.

He stared into the darkness, determined not to let his speed inch up. That was just fate tempting him. Fate trying to win the bet that he wouldn't — couldn't — succeed in becoming a better man.

"Sixty-five," he muttered aloud. "Keep it at sixty-fucking-five."

Saguaro cacti saluted him with stiff, prickly arms from both sides of the highway. When the road climbed steadily north, gaining altitude, they faded away along with the lights of Phoenix.

He was just starting up a steep incline when — *Vroom!* — a motorcycle roared by with a lean rider bent over the handlebars. A vintage Triumph, by the sound of it. And man, it actually hurt to watch something so beautiful move so fast.

That ought to be you, the dark voice goaded.

His inner wolf jumped out of a fitful snooze and howled in his mind. *Catch her. Catch her!*

Her?

He sniffed the air. The driver was a woman. Lean body, round hips. Perfect ass. Her leather boots laced up the back and ended in little tassels that whipped in the wind. A whiff of her scent teased his nose as she rushed by, and just like that, his body went from weary to full alert. Blood rushed through his veins, and every molecule in his body jumped up and down.

Get her! Earn her! Bring her back! his wolf screamed.

Up ahead, a truck was passing a slower camper, and the biker hung back just long enough for Luke to dream about catching up for a better look. But then the woman kicked the bike into another gear and shot into the suicidally narrow gap between the two vehicles.

Holy shit. Was she really going to try threading through that three-foot slot at ninety miles an hour?

The engine of her Triumph roared through the night, and his inner wolf whistled.

Holy shit. She really is.

His heart banged away as if he were the one pulling that crazy stunt.

The two vehicles lurched apart and horns blared, but she was already through the gap. A fist shook and horns cursed for another full minute, but the biker was long gone.

She was gone.

His wolf howled. Every nerve in his body tingled, and he leaned toward the open window, sucking in the last trace of her scent.

Red and blue lights flooded the road as a state trooper flashed past in pursuit of the biker. Luke grinned.

"Fly, baby. Fly," he whispered into the night.

He knew that high. That thrill that came from being chased. From knowing he'd get away, if only by the skin of his teeth. He nearly stomped on the gas to try to catch up, even though he had about as good a chance as that cop did. But he didn't because he was supposed to be through with all that.

So he forced himself to drive at that painfully slow pace, licking his lips against a parched feeling that hadn't been there before.

Her. His wolf sniffed the air. *Want her. Need her.*

"Sure, buddy." Luke snorted. "That's the last we'll ever see of her."

The second he said it, his chest started to ache, and his wolf threw its head up in a low, mournful howl. Like he'd just passed up the chance of his life or a lottery ticket had just cartwheeled past in the breeze and he hadn't even made a grab for it. Like destiny had flashed him a smile instead of a sneer for the first time ever, and he didn't even know how to react.

"Forget it." He slapped the wheel and straightened his shoulders. He needed to stick to his plan, not lust after a hot ass with a death wish. There was a reason he'd traded his old life for a beat-up old pickup and a crumpled map pointing the way north. The road home, if there still was such a place.

Well, the place was still there. Most of the people, too. That much, he'd heard through the shifter grapevine. But North Ridge, Colorado, had changed a lot since he'd left, and he had, too. Neither of them for the better.

Forgot about that. Speed up. We can still catch her, his wolf urged.

Luke shook his head. *Too late.*

He drove on, digesting the sinking feeling in his gut. Twenty miles later, he pulled off the highway at a floodlit crossroads with a gas station, a bar with a flashing Michelob sign, and not much else.

Ten beers on tap here at Louie's Bar, a sign blinked.

He licked his lips. Beer wasn't what he'd been thirsting for, but it wouldn't hurt.

Live music, the sign next to it announced.

Yeah, he could hear the country tune already, and it wasn't half bad.

Rooms, said another sign, though one of the two O's was out.

He could sleep in the back of the pickup, but a shave and a shower would help in the morning before his unannounced visit to Twin Moon pack — the one and only stop he'd planned between Phoenix and Colorado. There was still too much rogue in him to waltz right onto another wolf pack's turf and stand half a chance of avoiding a fight. And anyway, he'd already done enough fighting to last a lifetime.

So he pulled into the parking lot, stepped out of the truck, and entered the bar. At first sight, it was just like any other bar in any other two-horse town in Arizona. Same stale beer smell. Same sticky floor. Same dinged-up barstools, dim corners, and thrumming bass guitar. But one thing was different. One thing stood out like a rose among thorns.

Her. The blonde with the long legs standing at the bar.

Chapter Two

Luke spotted the woman the second she spotted him, and he tried tearing his eyes away. He really tried. But he couldn't. Just couldn't.

Her long legs tapered into leather boots with those damn tassels, teasing him. Golden hair cascaded over her shoulders. Bright blue eyes sparkled with mischief, after a split-second's pause in which he saw fear and loneliness. At least, he thought so. But that just went to show how she messed with his brain, because there was no way a woman like her would be acquainted with either of those emotions, right?

When their eyes locked, time stopped for a second — a full minute? an hour? — before lurching on. As if the earth had stopped spinning, and he and she were the only two who'd noticed. His heart stopped, too, and his whole body warmed.

Mine, his wolf hummed in a low, hungry tone.

Then, *whack!* The door swung shut, slamming Luke in the back.

He shook himself back to his senses. Whoa. Had time stopped or was that just him?

The hubbub of the bar went on without missing a beat. The singer was still crooning, a couple of out-of-step dancers still swaying, the waitresses still bustling through the Friday night crowd. But something in him felt different than before.

Her nostrils flared just like his did, testing the air.

Shifter, his brain said, recognizing the unmistakable scent of wolf.

Her! It's her! His wolf jumped up and down. *The daredevil on the bike.*

She broke into a grin, and he wondered if she'd heard. But even as a shifter, there was no way she could read his mind, just like there was no way he ought to be able to read hers.

Nope. No way he could hear her think something like, *Yum*, as she looked him over.

That had to be in his mind, or an assumption from the look in her eye. The one that definitely said, *Yum*.

There were about six guys fawning over her, one less worthy than the next, and Luke just about growled. Then someone stepped up, blocking his view, and he really did growl.

"Hold it," the bouncer said, eyeing Luke's tattoos and the scar that ran down his right arm. A three-hundred-plus-pound bouncer who bristled and stood at full height — a little shorter than Luke's six feet, but twice as wide.

Luke glared, and a second later, the bouncer wavered and stepped aside.

Yeah, that was the way it usually went. And a good thing, too, because his wolf was quick to rile up — and showing his secret side in a bar full of humans was never a good idea. Especially not with the leggy blonde looking at him like *that*.

She ignored the hungry huddle around her and stared at him.

His blood rushed. His heart rate tripled, and his inner wolf ordered him to march over and claim her as his own. Not as his own for the night, but really, truly, his own. Forever.

Mine! his wolf clamored. *Mate!*

And Jesus, what the hell was that all about?

Luke struggled to keep his crazy beast leashed. *Give it up, already.*

Will never let her go, his wolf declared.

He took her in for a moment longer, glued to those intense, flashing eyes that were even bluer than the tank top she wore, showing off an athletic figure. Proud, straight shoulders told the world she was no pushover. All feminine on top, all cowgirl below, with her worn jeans and leather boots.

His wolf whimpered, dreaming of touching her skin, of playing with her hair. Hair so rich and gold, he knew the color didn't come from a bottle. This woman was all natural, in every way.

All mine, his wolf growled so fiercely, he nearly gave in to the urge to stride over, glare the other guys off, and buy that woman a drink. They'd get to talking, then dancing, and before long, the two of them would head out the door to a more private place, like one of the rooms upstairs. Because he wanted her. *Needed* her like he'd never needed anything before.

So, go get her. To hell with that turning-over-a-new-leaf shit, the dark voice said.

He took one step forward, then pulled up short.

A month ago, he would have walked up to her without thinking. Hell, a week ago, too. But everything had changed in the intervening time. Ever since he'd heard the news from North Ridge, Colorado, a switch had flipped in him. It was time to man up and end his bad boy ways. Time to go home and help a struggling pack he'd turned his back on years ago.

Not time to fool around with a she-wolf, no matter how gorgeous she was.

So he put on his best poker face and sat at a table with his back to her. Better not send a hungry she-wolf the wrong signals.

But what if the signals are all right? his wolf protested.

"Can I get you a drink, honey?" the waitress leaned over, showing off her boobs. *A drink and anything else you want,* her body language said.

He didn't want anything else — unless that blonde was on the menu. He'd love that, but damn. Not tonight.

He ordered a beer and did his best to focus on the baseball game running on the TV. A minute later, he blinked and realized it was football.

So much for focusing on anything but the blonde.

Her scent teased him from across the room — even a room as pungent and crowded as this. He could feel her eyes on him. He could hear the vibration of her footsteps on the floor. Never mind the dozens of other feet clomping around the place — the light tap of hers stood out. And crap, she was coming his way. Didn't she know he had sworn off living close to the edge? Didn't she know he had a mission to fulfill?

Apparently not, because he sensed her approaching as if he'd known her his whole life. When she placed a hand on his shoulder and leaned close to his ear, long, silky locks tickled his cheek.

"Come and dance, stranger."

She had to shout above the music, but to him, it was a whisper, and her voice tangoed through his blood. Low. Sultry. Playful. And confident. Confident that she would get exactly what she wanted.

As in, him.

He gritted his teeth. It was a test. It had to be. Fate was checking how far it could push him before he gave in.

"Come and dance." She slid her fingers along his collar, featherlight.

Every other sound in the place faded. All he heard was her voice. All he *wanted* to hear was her voice.

"No thanks." He forced the words through his teeth.

Are you nuts? his wolf cried.

When she stepped in front of him and placed a hand on her hip, the background lights shot a halo through her hair.

Angel. Devil. Temptation on two feet.

She cocked her head, looking straight at him, and his jeans instantly grew tight. "You don't want to dance?"

"Believe me, I want to." Jesus, did he want. "But I can't."

She looked him up and down. Slowly. Torturously. Undressing him with eyes that flashed, telling him she liked what she found.

"Can't?" She tossed her hair. "You look pretty capable to me."

She leaned in to tease his collar again, and his eyes shut for a moment. God, how he'd like to show her how *capable* he was.

The sweet scent of arousal wrapped around him, and it wasn't just coming from her. His deeper, muskier scent was mixed in there, too, and it was all too easy to imagine getting naked with her.

"Shouldn't is more like it."

"Shouldn't?" She lifted one perfect eyebrow. Her hips swayed like she was already on the dance floor.

God, she made it so, so hard to remember all the reasons he had for being good.

Just say yes, his wolf said. *Yes, I want to dance.*

"Sorry," he said, gritting the words out over the *yes* poised on his tongue. A tongue he could already picture sliding over her lips. Parting them. Parting other sections of her body, too, and tasting her deep. Sliding along her—

He clenched his fists under the table and cleared his throat. "I'm turning over a new leaf."

"Ha." She laughed. "Try again."

He scowled. That was the hardest part about changing — getting other people to believe you. The biker pack he'd run with had thought he'd been joking, too.

"I mean it," he growled a little too fiercely.

That growl had shut up the meanest, ugliest, most brutal members of his old pack, but she didn't bat an eye.

She turned the closest chair around and straddled it. "Well, that sounds like a story I have to hear."

"Long story," he warned.

"Got plenty of time." She plucked the lime from the neck of his bottle, held it between her lips, and sucked.

The sparks that had been shooting around in his groin exploded into fireworks.

"I turned over a new leaf once," she mused.

"Yeah?"

She looked up. Wow. Did eyes really come in that bright a shade of blue?

"I gave it up after a day."

He grinned in spite of himself.

"Want to know the moral of the story?" She put both elbows on the table and leaned close. So close, he could smell the flowery scent of her shampoo. Her hair brushed his hands. He sat perfectly still, holding back a shiver of need.

"Moral?" That word, he hadn't had much use for over the past couple of years.

"The moral of the story is, you can't change who you really are, deep down inside."

Just what he was afraid of, not that he'd admit it, of course. And anyway, he got sidetracked, because there it was again — that flicker of fear and sadness in her eyes. Just a momentary flash that might have been his imagination. Must have been, because when he looked closer, she was all sass and confidence again.

"Why would a man like you want to turn over a new leaf?"

He pursed his lips. "Been bad."

She leaned closer, and the top of her peach-colored bra showed. "What if I like bad?"

Sweet Jesus, he was going to die from desire.

She dropped her voice and went on in a whisper. "After all, it's not often a she-wolf can find a guy capable of fulfilling her needs. On the dance floor, that is."

His cock swelled against the denim of his jeans. Yeah, he was capable, all right. And his wolf side was more than willing to indulge her in anything she desired. Still, he resisted, even though he could barely remember why any more. Hell, he could barely think.

Needs. We have needs, his wolf howled.

He'd never felt more twisted inside, like a whole wrestling match was going on inside his soul.

If she'd been human, he might have thought her a little too loose and easy. But shifters had a whole different level of sexual appetite, and she was simply going after what her wolf soul needed, just like he might if he wasn't trying to prove himself.

"Believe me, I wish I could. But I have to say no."

Her brow furrowed, telling him he was the first man who'd ever turned her down. He had to be, because who would be fool enough to reject a woman like her? The place was full of other candidates for her attention, all salivating over her every move.

She shrugged, wrapped a hand around his, and guided his beer bottle to her mouth. After a long, slow sip, she licked the foam off her lips.

"So, have you started?" she asked in a husky voice, still an inch away from his lips.

"Started what?" he asked a little breathlessly.

"Turning over that leaf."

Leaf? What leaf? His wolf wagged its tail.

"What do you mean?" he managed.

"Well, if you already turned it over — okay. I guess I'd better let you wallow in your lonely misery."

He hadn't been wallowing or lonely before he laid eyes on her, but suddenly, that was exactly how he felt.

Her face brightened, and she went on. "But if you were just *thinking* about a change, tomorrow would be just as good. Because tonight would definitely be more fun on the old side of the leaf. I guarantee it."

He leaned back and pointed at her with the one finger not wrapped around his bottle. "Anyone ever tell you you're a devil, sweetheart?"

She grinned a mile wide and blinked innocently. "Who, me?"

She's got a point, his wolf said. *We can start tomorrow.*

Was the beast kidding? He was supposed to be atoning for his sins.

"Why not start tomorrow?" she echoed.

On the other hand, maybe she was right. Tomorrow was just as good a time to become the new him. The haircut and vehicle trade didn't really count. Technically, he was still in the planning stages of a new life. One more night in his familiar old role — long nights in bars, fast bikes, and hard-hitting fights — wouldn't hurt, right?

Right! his wolf cheered.

She stood with a grin and stuck out her hand. No surprise there — she had a killer tight grip.

"I'm Carly. And you are?"

He hesitated. For years now, he'd been going by his road name. A name he'd been planning to drop along with his old ways. But if he wasn't quitting until tomorrow...

"Bones," he said, watching her eyes.

She lifted the other eyebrow and crossed her arms over her perfect rack. "I refuse to call a grown man Bones."

He crossed his arms right back. She wanted bad; he'd give it to her. "I refuse to go by any other name."

He waited for her reaction, then waited a little more. And... huh. She didn't give in. All the women he'd ever met in dim bars liked Bones. She didn't?

She looked him over again and pursed her lips. "Bruce."

He squinted at her against the light. She thought she could guess his name?

"Not Bruce. Bones."

She ignored that completely. "Chuck."

He shook his head.

"Rudy."

"Do I look like a Rudy?"

"Chip."

"Chip?"

"Okay... Homer?"

They both laughed at her wild guesses. His soul felt lighter, even if his balls grew tighter.

She went back to looking him up and down, studying him like a new species. Up, down, back again.

He grinned and leaned back in his chair, knowing she'd never guess. Which meant he'd finally chalk up a point over this she-devil.

After a pause of consideration, she nodded to herself and whispered, "Luke."

The front two legs of his chair tipped back to the floor with a jolt. Holy shit.

"Luke." She said it again, nodding like a mother who'd just found the perfect name for her son.

No one had called him Luke for a long, long time, and hearing it tugged on something inside. Like she'd snagged a little corner of the boy he'd once been and started reeling him out of where he'd been hiding, bit by bit. Or maybe it was the way she said it, like he was a goddamn saint or something.

"Luke." She smiled, proud of herself.

"Luke." He nodded, ceding her the point.

Carly and Luke. Sounds good together, his wolf decided.

Which was crazy. Since when was his wolf into that kind of thing?

Ever since we met her, the beast said, as if that were many happy years ago and not just a minute or two.

We didn't just meet her now. We saw her ages ago, on the highway.

On the highway, when she had passed in a blur?

I knew, the beast insisted. *I just knew.*

He didn't dare ask what the beast knew.

"Luke. Biblical name," Carly said with a naughty grin.

He laughed out loud. "Don't read into it."

"So, Luke," she said, teasing him all over again. "Wolf," she added in a lusty undertone too low for human ears. "You ready to dance?"

He considered for exactly two seconds before his resolve shattered. He shot to his feet, grabbed her hand, and pulled her close. So close, he wasn't breathing air, but her scent.

"Ready," he murmured, letting her lead the way.

Chapter Three

"You from around here?" Carly shouted over the music as she led her handsome stranger to the dance floor.

Yes, *her* stranger, at least for tonight.

Only tonight? her wolf cried.

Absolutely, positively, only for tonight, she shot back before the stupid beast got any bad ideas.

But it was too late, because her wolf had been entertaining bad ideas for a while. What was this obsession with settling down with a mate?

Every wolf needs a mate, the inner voice cried, so broken and lonely, Carly nearly caved in.

A second later, she straightened her shoulders and dug in her heels. No way would she give in to her wolf's silly desires. A woman who fell in love was far too likely to hand over her heart *and* her soul.

Think of Mom, she told her wolf.

You're not her, the wolf whined back. *You're you. You're strong.*

Yes, she was strong, but so had her mother been once upon a time. And Carly had no desire to turn out the same way.

Her wolf licked its lips and tried a different tack. *He's gorgeous. Just give him a chance.*

That, she fully intended to. One chance for one night, but not a second more. Just like all the other men she'd picked up over the last few years. She'd allow herself one night of fun, of satisfying her body's needs — and then forget about him. It was better that way.

Not better, her wolf whined. *Lonelier. And this man is different.*

That much, she had to agree with. There *was* something different about him. Something she couldn't put her finger on. Sure, she'd picked up a hunk or two — or ten — in the past and made sure she got exactly what she wanted for exactly one night. But she'd never come on as strong, as fast, as pit-bull determined as just now. Why did she crave this man so much?

He's dangerous, her wolf hummed. Not in warning — in glee.

But that didn't explain it, either. She'd done bad boy types brimming with anger, ink, and attitude. She'd done broody road warriors. What was it with this guy?

Mate, her wolf whispered. *Mine.*

When Luke shook his head, the light cast shadows over high cheekbones, and she wondered if he'd read her mind. But no, he was just answering her question. Was he from around here?

"Just passing through. How about you?"

The man had a voice that made her toes curl. A body a sculptor would pay to shape. A face any woman would fall in love with. He was the perfect combination of rugged and handsome, like a cowboy from a cigarette ad crossed with a model for a fancy cologne. She sniffed deeply, and her inner wolf sighed.

Mine.

Just for tonight, she reminded her wolf. Then she shut it in its inner cage and let herself drink the man in.

His short, dark hair stuck up a little at the front. His deep, dark tan was closer to a windburn, like a hardcore biker who'd spent most of his life on the road. Dozens of small scars hinted at a lot of midnight brawls, and the bigger ones — like the scar that zigzagged down his right arm — spoke of life-or-death shifter fights. His piercingly dark eyes carried a little bit of everything. Love. Hate. Betrayal. Burning anger. A sprinkle of hope.

She looked a little deeper and found joy, hiding all the way in the back. A bridled kind of joy just waiting for its chance.

And fear? Not a trace.

She licked her lips. No self-respecting member of her family would approve of her messing with a transient, bad boy type.

A man with big, bold tattoos who stood for everything they despised.

Forbidden, in other words. The best kind.

He looked at her expectantly, and she realized she hadn't answered his question. Was she from around here?

Sort of. Kind of. A long story she really didn't have time to explain. *I'm a member of two packs — Arroyo Hills in California, where I grew up with my loony mother, and Twin Moon Ranch, where my father and siblings live. It's just up the road from here, and it's paradise, only I never get to stay there long. I'm always in between.*

But that would be the wimpy side of her soul talking, so she quickly tucked the thoughts away.

"Just visiting," she said.

Luke nodded, looking as relieved as she was. If he was just passing through, this would be easy. A fun night of dancing followed by more intimate moves once she got him somewhere private, and then in the morning, a quick thanks and good-bye. That was her *modus operandi* when it came to men. Easy come, easy go. Quick. Convenient. Fun.

And never, ever anything deeper than that.

Never? her wolf whimpered.

She shook her head firmly. Thank goodness for her tough human side. It was her inner wolf who deluded itself with visions of the perfect man — or even worse, the perfect mate.

It would be nice to have a mate, her wolf whimpered.

Like that ass, Craig? she shot back.

Her inner wolf all but bared its teeth. *Never. That was not my idea.*

Carly took another gulp of beer, trying to purge the memory from her mind. Her home pack had actually welcomed Craig in and encouraged the idea of a mating to him.

Just get to know him a little, her mother had urged.

Like Carly needed more than one glance to see through the man with slicked-back hair and a cocky grin. Craig was arrogant. Selfish. Ambitious, too — dangerously so.

Gonna find me a good pack to lead, you know, Craig had declared. *And I need a good she-wolf at my side.*

More like a she-wolf at his beck and call, Carly figured. He'd barely even looked at her, addressing the Arroyo Hills alpha instead.

He's perfect for you, her mother had declared.

Perfect? Carly could barely stand the overwhelming scent of Craig's hair gel, let alone the rest of him.

Luckily, her home pack was progressive enough not to force anything on her. But they sure as hell could pressure her. After three days of that, she'd hit the road, heading to her father's side of the family at Twin Moon Ranch for a little reprieve.

This man isn't like Craig, her wolf murmured about Luke. *This man is perfect.*

Carly considered. The perfect man was one she could wave good-bye to on her way out of town. And that made Luke Mr. Perfect, if only for tonight.

Luke smiled one of those killer smiles, and though she melted inside, she made sure to shoot her best grin back. The one that said, *I want you to know, Hot Stuff, that as much as you think you're playing me, I'm playing you.*

I know, his eyes twinkled. *Believe me, I know.*

"So, no hurry to get anywhere tonight?" he asked.

She grinned. "No hurry."

Twin Moon Ranch was just up the road, but her family wasn't expecting her at any particular time. And the second she stepped foot on the ranch, she could forget about this kind of fun. Her dad was the former alpha of that wolf pack, and her brother the current leader. That made fooling around with any male in the pack out of the question. It was just too complicated. So a night with Luke was exactly what she needed to tide her over until she could hit the road again.

Definitely not in a hurry, her wolf murmured.

Not with the dance floor just livening up. And certainly not after she'd spotted Hot Stuff eyeing her up and down. When she'd sniffed and caught the scent of wolf...

Yum. Her inner beast practically purred as she led him closer to the band.

The minute they hit the dance floor, he pulled her close, and hot damn, did that he-wolf have moves. Luke led her around the floor like she hadn't been led — or allowed herself to be — in a long time, sweeping her in and out of his arms in glorious twists and turns. It was like dancing with sunshine, even though they were in a seedy bar at the stroke of midnight.

"Promise me something," she said the next time he pulled her into his chest.

"What's that?" He grinned, all bad boy again.

"Promise that turning over a new leaf doesn't mean you're going to give up dancing."

His hearty laugh filled his tanned face with a new glow. "I guess I have plenty of other sins to give up first."

Just hearing the word *sin* made her inner temperature shoot up another few degrees. And when he said *give up*, he held her closer, as if that were the last thing he wanted to do.

Maybe he wasn't really ready to give up all his sins.

Maybe he shouldn't even try.

Maybe a girl like her was exactly what this man needed to hang on to all the good parts of being bad.

"You know that line, right?" she asked. "The one about laughing with sinners instead of crying with saints."

The music slowed just then, and his face grew somber. "Done plenty of laughing," he said, so quietly she almost missed the words. "And not always at the right thing."

Regret had its own signature scent, and it snuck into the space around him. A lot of regret, it seemed. It clouded his eyes and slowed his step.

"Still beats crying," she said. "Come on, Hot Stuff. That leaf's not going anywhere before tomorrow." She pulled him through the next couple of moves until he found his rhythm again.

"I guess not," he admitted, taking the lead once more.

The band followed up with another fast song, and before long, all those bumps, touches, and grinds filled her mind with visions of what else she could do with this man and how good it would be. Then the band transitioned into one of those slow love songs made just for a woman in her mood. The kind that gave her a chance to sniff his neck up close, to let her hands trace the muscles of his back. Which meant a hell of a lot of tracing while she squeezed her chest and hips against his. He smelled like leather and fresh air and the open road. And Jesus, did he turn her on. Those dark, hungry eyes — Black eyes? Brown? — so focused on hers. The easy way their bodies pressed closer with each beat.

His hands played over her ribs, but just when they got deliciously close to where she really wanted to feel them, he backed away.

"Hey," she protested, clamping her hands over his. She tugged them up until he was cupping the lower edge of her breasts. Not high enough to give the crowd a real show, but enough to make her intentions clear.

"Don't stop," she whispered. And drat, it came out sounding much needier than she intended.

"Wasn't planning to," he whispered, pulling her hips against his.

"So what exactly were you planning?" she teased.

He pursed his lips, but his eyes gave him away. They sparked and smoldered as they took her in. Yeah, Hot Stuff wanted her, all right.

The music sped up again, and she made sure every step led them closer to the door.

"Tired of dancing?" Now he was the tease.

She let her hands slide far enough down the back of his jeans to answer. "Just ready to move this dance somewhere else. Somewhere private. Are you with me, bad boy?"

His eyes had that feral wolf glow, and he nodded once. "I think they have rooms upstairs."

"I think I might not make it that far."

"Good," he said, leaning in close to whisper in her ear. "Then I get to tease you a while, too."

Wait a minute. Teasing was her job.

But he was already pulling her along. He detoured to the bar just long enough to pick up a key to a room, then led her out the door.

"Perfect night for a—" he started.

The second they stepped into the cool night air, she hustled him against the wall and covered his mouth in a deep, hungry kiss. A sloppy kiss, with her tongue and hands all over the place, caught up in a sudden craving for this man.

Want him. Need him, her wolf cried.

Her kiss was wild. Hungry. Starving, almost.

Luke's lips moved under hers just as eagerly — but tenderly, too. It was in the way he threaded his fingers through her hair. The way his thumbs stroked her cheeks. The way his lips slowed hers down to stretch out the moment.

What bad boy had ever kissed her like this? A kiss that gave instead of taking. A kiss full of yearning and shattered dreams.

He needs us, her wolf said. *And we need him.*

She pushed those thoughts away and concentrated on the physical. Her body screamed for his touch, his heat. Outside. Inside.

Deep, deep inside, her wolf hummed.

A sentiment he must have read on her mind, because he growled.

She ran a hand down the hard planes of his chest and stomach to the bulge in his jeans and palmed him until he did it again. A real, bone-deep growl.

"Watch what you wish for, she-wolf."

"Is that a warning or a promise?"

"Both." He tipped her head to the side and started kissing her neck. Soft, hard, then soft again.

"Luke," she whispered, clawing at his shirt.

He backed her against the wall and spread her legs with his. Nipping and licking and promising her the night of her life. He groaned her name in his mind.

Carly. Carly. Carly...

Wait. She was just imagining that, right?

"Upstairs, bad boy," she said, grabbing him by the collar. She led him to the second floor, where they kissed and groped their way to the third room down. By the time he slammed the door closed and pinned her against it, she was panting.

"Gotta get this off," she breathed, yanking his shirt over his head.

"This, too," he said, smoothing his hands up her body until her shirt fluttered away.

The more layers she helped him out of, the more ink she revealed. The man had tattoos everywhere. Tribal swirls on his shoulders, jagged lightning strikes down his arms. They accentuated all that muscle, that bulk.

Within seconds, most of her clothes were strewn around the room, and her panties were down around her ankles. She kicked them off and fumbled with his jeans.

"Bye-bye, boxers," she murmured, wondering what pattern she might uncover next.

Shouldn't go this fast, a corner of her mind said. *Shouldn't feel so drunk with desire.*

It shouldn't feel like her first time either, but it did. The sparks shooting through her veins, the anticipation. Hunger mixed with a tiny bit of fear — the kind of fear that went with handing over trust. Of being pushed past the edge of what she could control.

Her wolf howled deliriously, and she tried to leash it in. But then Luke dropped to his knees in front of her, spread her legs, and looked up.

Oh, yes, both sides of her soul moaned at the same time.

Luke didn't utter a word, but his eyes glowed. And shit, not just with arousal, but with that possessive, *my-woman* look her brothers gave their mates.

The scary thing was, she was pretty sure her eyes were glowing the same way.

When he slid his thumbs down her center line, tipped forward to spread her wider, and began to feast, every note of caution fled her mind. Words caught in her throat as he ravaged her body in the most delicious way. With his tongue. His fingers. His searingly hot breath. She clutched at the door, his hair, then his shoulders as he pushed her closer and closer toward a shattering orgasm.

Come for me, his voice sounded in her mind. Coaxing, not commanding. Begging, almost.

She tipped her head against the door, moaning as her muscles clenched tighter. She was definitely hearing things. Only packmates could hear each other's thoughts.

Packmates and destined mates, her wolf said.

Not going there, she moaned, trying to hang on to her last scrap of control. *So not going there.*

Mates, her wolf sang.

She wanted to protest, but she couldn't. Not with a tornado of need whipping through her soul.

Come for me, Luke murmured, swirling his tongue against her clit while his fingers tickled her inside.

She cried out as the orgasm shook through her. The room was dark, but her vision filled with light. Her ears filled with the sound of her own moans.

"Yes...yes..." she cried.

Was this really happening? She'd never let a man take full charge of her body before. She'd always kept her defenses firmly up. What was wrong with her?

She shuddered, succumbing to the rushing wave of need. Not sure which way was up or down. No longer caring as long as that exquisite pleasure never ebbed.

"Yes..."

She rode the high for another full minute then went limp against the wall, panting hard.

Amazing, she swore she heard Luke humming in her mind. He scrubbed his stubbly chin against her thigh, marking her as his.

His fingers tightened around her hips, anchoring her until her senses snapped back into place. Well, only half her senses — the ones controlled by her wolf.

Need this man, it cried. *Need my mate.*

Before she knew it, she was hauling him over to the bed and straddling him. Lowering her body over his thick, hard shaft one agonizingly perfect inch at a time. She groaned, relishing the inner stretch, the heat. Then she started rocking. Faster and faster still until they were both bucking wildly.

"Luke..."

His name slipped far too easily from her tongue. Her heart beat far too quickly for a woman who ought to be guarding her soul, and her pulse skipped too erratically for a person pretending to be in control.

"Turn," he murmured, all low and growly.

She rolled, letting him take the top without so much as a sassy comment.

"More," she begged. *Begged*, damn it, while her wolf howled and her legs tightened around his waist.

Sex as she'd always known it was a game, a short-term distraction. Sex was supposed to be about her toying with a man who might satisfy her for a little while.

Then this must not be sex, her wolf growled.

This was all-encompassing. Breathtaking. Soul-wrenching. This was pure emotion, knocking reason aside and stealing her control.

Luke's eyes flashed, telling her it was the same for him. A first. A last, maybe. A totally new sensation. He slowed just long enough to pull her hips high, and she practically sang as he thrust into her again.

Yes was the only word she could manage, so she panted it. Screamed it. Scratched it into his sides as he pounded into her again and again.

"Yes," she moaned when she thought it couldn't get any better. But then he pushed even harder, and the wave inside her crashed, toppling her over the edge.

She cried out, shuddering with a mighty orgasm.

He grunted and tipped his head back, going perfectly still as his own release hit.

Mine, her wolf howled, relishing the hot burn of his come deep inside her body. *Mine. Mine. Mine.*

"Yes," she panted, pretending *yes* meant *Oh, that's good* and not, *Yes, he's mine.* But the line of meaning kept blurring, even in her own mind.

"Whoa," she whispered, going limp all over.

"So good," he murmured as they lay close and sweaty on the bed.

Sure is, her wolf hummed inside as Luke scrubbed his chin against her cheek, marking her as his.

Chapter Four

Luke panted into the sheets, unable to process any words other than two.

Holy shit.

He sank back onto the mattress, in no hurry to go anywhere or to think anything except *holy shit* over and over again.

And, crap. Now he was snuggling against this woman like she was his goddamn teddy bear. What was he thinking, stroking her hair back to stare into her eyes and whispering her name?

"Carly," he murmured, again and again.

Damn it, he never did that, because a name made a person real. A name gave a person meaning. A name was the key to a person's soul.

"Luke," she whispered.

She might as well have puffed into the glowing embers of a fire, because a wave of heat swept through his body. He hadn't gone by Luke in years, and it made him feel like a different man. A better man, almost.

A fucked-up man, he decided, cradling her body against his.

Mine, his wolf growled. *Just listen.*

Listen to her heart tap against his chest?

No, dummy. Listen.

He heard a whisper on the wind. A low sound that could have been a chuckle — or a warning. What was that?

That's destiny.

Destiny?

Destiny. His wolf nodded firmly. *That's destiny, telling us she's our mate.*

The idea ought to have made him run for the hills, but all he felt was Carly's sweet heat.

She sighed, and he wondered if she'd heard it, too. But then she snuggled closer and shut her eyes.

He did, too. Her hair was soft on his shoulder, her breath light on his neck. It slowed and evened out as she fell asleep.

He counted to ten, figuring it was time to pull his usual trick — namely, easing out of a woman's embrace. Step two would be to collect his things quietly, and step three would be to slip away. It was easier on everyone that way.

But he couldn't break away, not when he'd counted to ten or twenty or even one hundred. He didn't *want* to break away or fumble his jeans on. He wanted to stay.

And stay and stay and stay, his wolf agreed.

Finding a willing woman was easy. But finding this sense of satisfaction or peace… not so much. This inner calm, this balance. Why rush away from this bliss?

His own breathing slowed, and the time between beats of his heart quieted, too. His whole soul calmed in a way it hadn't dared in years, and he fell asleep.

A deep, drugged sleep from which he woke a few times — or dreamed about waking. Once, Carly woke him hungry for more, and he was happy to oblige. Another time, it was him, unable to keep his hands off her and waking her by mistake. One thing led to another, and they tumbled right into another sizzling round of sex. The third time he awoke, it wasn't to do anything much but to stare into those amazing blue eyes. Well, he stared into her eyes. She studied his tattoos.

Just about every woman he'd ever slept with did that, but Carly did it differently. She didn't trace the ink so much as the space between the lines, and when she tilted her head, it was as if she could see past all those markings to the person he'd once been.

"Luke," she whispered then paused.

He strained to hear what she might say next. Would it be, *Luke, I've never felt this way before?*

Because damn, he sure as hell never had. So warm. So happy. So close to something great.

Or would she say, *Luke, we need to talk?*

Talking would be okay, too. Because he couldn't decode the sparks in her eyes, and he was dying to know what they meant.

"Luke," she whispered as the first pink streak of dawn inched over her skin.

He leaned closer, nodding eagerly.

Her eyes flickered with some inner battle before she gulped and sighed. "I have to go."

His wolf howled as he forced himself to say, "Me, too."

But neither of them budged except for inching closer.

"Soon," she said, kissing his jaw.

"Real soon," he agreed, working his lips down the amazing curves of her body again.

His wolf side took over from there, and all he could do was witness Carly come undone all over again. Just like him, damn it. Just like him.

He didn't remember who fell asleep first, but he knew who was the first to wake up the next morning. Carly. He could tell by the sound of her Triumph roaring down the road.

"Whoa. Wait!" He ran out of the room just in time to see her rev the engine and whip around a corner, ready to burn up the road.

No! his wolf cried.

The roar of the Triumph's engine faded before being erased by the rumble of an eighteen-wheeler that shot past, also heading north.

He stood buck naked on the balcony above the bar, gripping the railing. Forcing himself not to take chase.

What a woman, his wolf murmured in his head. *What a night.*

He shook his head. What a foreign feeling not to want to let her go.

He sniffed the air. Last night, each breath he inhaled had been cool and full of promise. Now the air was as parched and lifeless as the landscape.

She's heading north. The way we're going, right? his wolf asked, full of hope. Far, far too much hope.

He shook his head as if to clear his ears of the suggestion. What he really needed was to scrub his entire memory of her. He had to get his head screwed back on. He was a man on a mission, not some rogue just dicking around.

There was so much more I wanted to do, his wolf cried. *To say. To hear. To share.*

He headed back into the dim room and looked around, telling himself it was all good. Washing his face didn't help, so he showered and scrubbed, too, trying to rub Carly's scent off, because even the faintest whiff of it drove him crazy with a desperate need. When he stepped back into the bedroom to collect his clothes, he took a deep sniff in spite of himself, catching the last of her scent. Then he picked every item slowly off the floor. Jeans. Boxers. Shirt. Boots. Jacket…

He looked around. Wait. Where was his leather jacket?

Had he left it in the bar? In his sad excuse for four wheels? He checked all over for the only relic of his past he'd wanted to hold on to, then stood beside his truck, sniffing the breeze. Then he cracked into a wide grin, realizing where it had gone.

Carly had taken it. He replayed the fleeting memory of her rounding the corner on her Triumph. Yeah, she'd taken his jacket — along with a piece of his heart. Which meant she wanted to hang on to the memory of their night, too.

Then he caught himself. Damn. He needed to lose those memories, not hang on to them.

He kicked the dirt, feeling an unfamiliar ache in his chest.

The ache in my heart, his wolf sniffed.

Well, maybe that was a good thing. It proved there was something left of his heart after all those years of drunken brawls and battles for no particular cause.

It hurts, his wolf complained.

He paid his bill — because he really was turning over a new leaf now — asked for directions to Twin Moon Ranch, and headed north. A few miles later, he spotted the knotted old carcass of a tree that had been struck by lightning ages ago — the landmark he'd been told about. He pulled off the highway and slowed to a stop, eyeing the dirt road ahead.

Should he, or shouldn't he?

Highway traffic whipped past, tempting him to zoom onward, too.

If we keep heading north, we might catch up to Carly, his wolf urged.

His grip on the steering wheel tightened. He sniffed the air for the scent of wolf, but the desert air was too dry. The stiff, prickly leaves of the surrounding brush swayed in the wind, teasing him.

Why bother stopping at a pack of strangers? And for what? Why was it so important to say thank you to a man he'd never met?

He gritted his teeth. Because it was the right thing to do.

The dirt road to the ranch twisted and turned, hiding the future from him, and Carly's voice whispered through his mind. *Why turn over a new leaf?*

Yeah, his wolf demanded. *Why?*

He didn't really have to change. He could just head to Colorado and...and...

And look his family in the face? No, he had to see his plan through. And it all started with this small step.

"All right, already," he murmured to himself, forcing his eyes ahead.

The truck groaned over the bumpy dirt road, urging him to turn back. But as powerful as the pull north was, the pull toward the ranch was even stronger. As if fate was leaning in, saying, *You really need to go this way.*

The truck rattled onward for a couple of miles, and he wondered who the hell would live way out in the middle of these scrubby plains. His home territory in North Ridge, Colorado had been remote, too, like most wolf packs preferred, but it was surrounded by thick woods, mighty mountains, and roaring rivers. A beautiful place.

The morning air wafted in through the open window, trying to convince him that Arizona had its own brand of beauty. A harsher, edgier kind, with red rock mesas and rolling hills. A breeze ruffled the scrublands. A brown bird flitted between the bushes then disappeared. When he slowed down to lurch over a gulley, a sprinkle of red against dun-colored earth caught his gaze — a row of tiny red flowers hung like upside-down tea cups from a single stem. The kind of flower he'd be tempted to pick for Carly if he ever got to see her again.

He gripped the wheel a little harder and shook his head. "Focus, damn it. Focus."

The road forked, then led over a dry creek and finally under a timber gateway hung with an honest to God old-fashioned cattle brand — two circles, overlapping by a third.

"Twin Moon Ranch," he murmured, taking a deep breath.

The place had developed quite a reputation over the past few years. The new powerhouse among shifter packs in the West, everyone said. Even the rough, tough drifter pack he'd led had kept a respectful distance from the place.

He parked his truck just outside the gateway and slid out, careful to keep his hands in plain view.

"Hello?"

The ranch was quiet. Eerily so.

Two rows of false-fronted buildings hemmed in a wide, dusty lane. A pinto stood tied to a hitching post, quietly swishing its tail in the shade of mighty cottonwood trees. Brownish-green leaves rustled overhead, and that was about the only sound except for the hurried footsteps of a kid who'd bolted the second he spotted Luke.

"Hello?" Luke called.

It was just like one of those Wild West movie scenes when a stranger arrives in a town and finds the place quiet. Too quiet. Luke looked around, half expecting a dozen cowboys to come rushing out, each aiming a Colt .45 at his head.

Footsteps sounded behind him, and he whirled.

Chapter Five

"Howdy," a voice rang out. The voice was friendly but guarded; chipper yet wary.

Luke turned as a man stepped out from between two buildings. A man nothing like what he expected, because he didn't look so much like a cowboy as a surfer dude with scrappy blond hair and a million-dollar smile.

"Can I help you?" surfer-dude asked.

Can I help you? had *What the hell are you doing here?* coded between the lines, but the guy seemed to be withholding judgment. For now.

"Luke Brandstetter." His tongue nearly tripped over the sound of his own name.

"Cody Hawthorne," the man said, shaking Luke's hand with a tight grip that said, *I'd love to trust you, but I don't. Not one bit.* Then he smiled in a way that meant, *Don't take it personally.*

Luke immediately liked the man. And hell, he was impressed that the guy hadn't already called out half a dozen thugs to back him up.

Maybe the new haircut was working. Or maybe this guy was just supremely confident in his own fighting skills. Either way, Luke wasn't here for a fight, and he made that clear, keeping his hands loose instead of locked into fists.

"I'm looking for Kyle Williams," he said.

Surfer-dude — er, Cody — looked him up and down. "And what would you want with Kyle?"

He took a deep breath because, whoa — the moment he'd been thinking about for a long, long time had finally come. The first step on the long road home.

"I heard he killed Greer Steton of North Ridge pack." Luke just about spat the name out along with the bitter aftertaste it brought.

Cody Hawthorne tilted his head. "Greer Steton was a bastard son of a bitch who didn't deserve the title of alpha. You got a problem with that?"

No, he didn't have a problem with that, except for wishing he'd been the one to do the deed. "That bastard son of a bitch, Greer, killed my father. My uncle. My older brother."

As he said the words, images he'd locked away years ago came flooding back. He saw the slow, torturous deaths of his loved ones, strung up as a warning to anyone who dared to stand up to Greer's despotic regime.

He remembered it all, right down to his mother screaming, *Run, Luke. Run!*

Just thinking about it made him sick. He'd wanted to stand and fight with the others, but he'd been only fourteen.

Run, Luke. Run.

He swallowed hard. Yes, he had run. Long and hard until he was miles from North Ridge. He'd eked out a living on the streets until he fell in with one band of rogues — then another, and another until he saw himself as one of them and not a member of a once-proud pack brought to its knees.

He cleared his throat and blinked into the sunlight filtering through the trees. He'd been running for too many years. Blocking out the ugly parts of his past — especially the ugliest part, which he couldn't even bring himself to say. Not to this stranger. Not here. Not now.

"I came to thank Kyle Williams for killing Greer." The memories put a shake in his voice, so he coughed and made sure the rest came out firmly. "That's all I want here. Just to say thank you. Then I'll be on my way."

Cody's gaze softened a bit. Did he know the horrors Greer had inflicted on the wolves of North Ridge pack? Could he imagine what abuses Luke's mother and sister had been subjected to?

"Then you'll be on your way where?"

Luke very nearly retorted with a *None of your goddamned business,* but he reined it in. This was day one in his new life. He wasn't a rogue any more, which meant he had to ask nicely for what he wanted instead of just taking it.

"North Ridge."

Cody's eyes narrowed. Could a guy from a quiet backwater like Twin Moon Ranch understand what it was like, coming from a messed-up place like North Ridge?

"And what exactly do you plan to do there?"

A good question. Luke wasn't so sure himself. The oldest of his uncles had been alpha of North Ridge pack until Greer came along, and Luke sometimes found himself entertaining notions of taking on the role himself. Over the years, he'd worked up the hierarchy of the rogue pack until he was top dog. He'd whipped a scrappy band of rogues into an organized and relatively civil group of drifters. Oh, they had their wild ways, but the meaningless violence and random attacks were a thing of the past.

So, yeah. He could lead a pack. But did he want to?

He cleared his throat and kept his answer as vague as his plans. "I just want to help get the pack back on its feet. To do what I should have done years ago."

"And what's that?"

"Find my mother. My relatives. Help them get their lives back together." He shrugged, trying to push unfamiliar emotions away.

A long, quiet minute ticked by in which Luke didn't trust himself to say much else. He'd forgotten how much the memories hurt. Forgetting — or pretending to forget — was so much easier, but he'd done enough of that.

Cody nodded. "Tell you what. I'll walk you to Kyle's house myself."

And off they went, a couple of wolves — perfect strangers who had no real reason to trust each other except the honesty in each other's voices — strolling side by side like that happened every day.

Which was crazy because, in most places, shifters didn't welcome strangers onto their home turf. They didn't help them come to terms with their own demons. At least, none of the shifters Luke knew. Not the wolves, not the bears he'd met, and definitely not the cougars.

Luke looked around. Maybe these wolves were different. Maybe they valued peace along with prosperity and defending their home turf. Maybe this place was as special as the rumors said.

Cody led him past tidy homes and stepped over an irrigation ditch gurgling with water that nourished lush lawns. The winter sun shone, and it was nippy at this high altitude, but it still felt good to walk in the shade. People waved at Cody and gave Luke polite nods. Two little girls whizzed by on bikes, and a big black dog loped after them with his tongue hanging out the side of his mouth.

"Hi, Daddy!" one yelled.

"Hi, sweetie." Cody waved.

It was like the best parts of Luke's memories — the ones that stretched from before Greer's arrival at North Ridge — all jumped out of nowhere and replayed themselves in front of his eyes. Which was weird, because he never really thought of them as memories. More like fantasies of how life could have been.

"Has Twin Moon Ranch always been like this?" he couldn't help asking. Almost whispering.

"Like what?" Cody asked, not even turning around.

"This... nice. This quiet. This... safe."

Cody laughed. "Not when I was a kid. But the last couple of years have been good ones." He waved a hand in the direction the kids had gone. "And we'll make sure it stays that way."

Cody left out the firm *damn it* that punctuated his sentence, but it wasn't necessary. The determination was palpable in the man's voice, as was the *We worked our asses off to make it this way.*

Luke looked around, wondering if it would be possible to bring serenity to a place as brutalized as North Ridge. He was ready to work his ass off, for sure. But would the wolves of

North Ridge pack welcome him? Would anyone even recognize him?

He straightened his shoulders. Those were questions for later. Right now, Cody was leading him up to a house that stood behind a little rise, away from the rest. A place with new windows and a new porch and a lawn so green it had to be young — like the family that inhabited the place, judging by the toys littering the grass.

Cody didn't knock on the door. He hollered. "Hey, Kyle. Hey, Stef. I got someone who wants to meet you."

A young woman came to the door holding a toddler on her hip. A cute little guy with spiky brown hair. "Hi," she said, looking from Cody to Luke.

Luke wished he had a hat to tip to her the way Cody did.

"Hi," he settled for saying as politely as he possibly could.

The woman called over her shoulder. "You coming, Kyle?"

A shadow moved in the hallway behind her, and Luke stuck out his hand, ready to greet the man who'd rid the world of a true beast.

"Kyle, this is Luke Brandst—" Cody started before the peaceful scene exploded into chaos.

An ear-splitting roar cut through the air. A scream followed. Everything blurred, and Luke was slammed into the ground by a heavy weight. The world turned into a flurry of shouts and flailing limbs.

"No. Kyle, no!" the woman screamed.

Luke stuck out his hands. He was flat on his back in the gravel pathway with a furious wolf poised, ready to tear his throat out. He was fast, but damn, this Kyle guy was a tornado.

"Daddy! Daddy!" the kid bawled.

"Hold it, Kyle!" Cody shouted.

You will die, the wolf poised above him said with a clack of its teeth.

Luke held perfectly still as the wolf's saliva dripped onto his cheek, slowly processing what had happened. The guy who'd come to the door with a relaxed, curious look had shifted into wolf form and attacked him out of the blue.

Luke stuck his hands up. "Whoa. Take it easy. What did I do?"

The wolf was so close, Luke couldn't help but inhale its scent. Something about it seemed familiar, somehow. But how?

"He's who?" the woman yelped, looking at the wolf. She scooped her son closer and scuttled back a few steps, glaring at Luke.

What the hell was going on?

"What? Who is he?" Cody asked the wolf.

The wolf — Kyle — was too busy snarling to answer. But slowly, a vague picture formed in Luke's mind — a picture of a bar in some godforsaken corner of the earth that he'd stopped at years ago. That was back in his time with a biker gang he'd briefly joined at the peak of their wildest days. A couple of rednecks had picked a fight with one of the gang members, and a brawl had broken out. The cops had showed up and—

Oh, shit.

At the very moment that Luke remembered what had happened, Cody cried out to Kyle.

"What? This is the guy who attacked you?"

"Wait," Luke tried, but the wolf above him kept snarling.

Fuck, fuck, fuck. How was he supposed to know Kyle was the very guy he'd accidentally clawed in that brawl so long ago? The wound had been deep enough to turn the human into a wolf shifter in a slow, excruciating process that few men survived.

Well, this guy had survived, all right. And boy, was he pissed.

Luke kept his hands up. The alpha side of his soul demanded that he fight back, but he resisted. He'd resolved to own up to his past and damn it, this ugly surprise was part of the process. The first and possibly last part, given how close the points of those fangs were to his throat.

Kyle growled ominously, eyeing Luke's neck.

"Daddy! Daddy!" came a terrified squeal, making the wolf pause. A second later, the growl resumed, but on a different note. Not so much a *prepare to die* growl as a *wait till I get you out of sight of my family* sound that promised a slow, painful death.

The woman — Stef — stepped forward. Even though the massive wolf spat and growled and showed a hell of a lot of white, she showed no fear. She stroked Kyle's coat, murmured in a low voice, and clutched at his ruff.

Finally, with a vicious bark inserted into his growl, Kyle lifted his muzzle clear of Luke's throat and stepped back. He shook with fury and kept one step ahead of his mate, shielding her body with his.

Luke wanted to protest. He wasn't here to threaten a woman or to terrorize a kid.

You sure as hell did bring it upon yourself, though, a dark voice in the back of his mind said.

"Okay, Kyle, we got this," Cody tried, and though his voice was silk over the turbulence of the scene, Kyle aimed another defiant snap in Luke's direction.

Footsteps thumped along the path as two men ran into the yard.

"What the hell is going on?" one of them thundered. The pack alpha. It had to be.

Kyle, still in wolf form, twitched his tail in fury, and Luke rolled away. Yeah, it was pretty damn clear who was crawling away from whom here, and he didn't like that one bit.

Turning over a new leaf, he told himself over and over. *Turning over a new leaf.*

But, man. Who knew it could be so hard to do such a simple thing?

The newcomers yanked Luke unceremoniously to his feet.

"Who the hell are you?" the tall, dark, and dangerous one thundered, shaking him.

The spiky-haired wolf paced, swinging its head in an angry arc, guarding his family.

The sight of the terrified kid hiding behind the mom made Luke sick. The child looked at him as if he were a monster. Exactly the way Luke had looked at Greer, once upon a time.

"Fucking Greer," he cursed under his breath so the kid didn't hear. He already had plenty of reasons to make good on the mess that was his past, but now he had another one. He would make something of himself, damn it, so that kids would look up at him with respect and not fear. He'd amass enough good deeds to overwrite all the crap he'd been known for up to then.

He'd do all that — if these wolves let him off Twin Moon Ranch alive and unskinned.

"Take him to the council house," Cody said, exchanging looks with the alpha.

The two men hauled him off, all the way back across the ranch and up a couple of stairs. Then they threw him through a doorway into a building. He skidded across the wooden floor, scraping every inch of exposed skin raw until he came to rest against someone's foot.

"Hey," a woman yelped, stepping back.

It took a minute for his eyes to adjust to the dim light — a minute in which several pairs of heavy boots clomped across the floor, making him wonder if they'd hauled him inside to talk or to beat the crap out of him.

He looked up — and up and up. A long way up a familiar pair of lean legs clad in leather boots. Scuffed leather boots with laces that ended in little tassels tied high and at the back.

Oh, shit.

He knew those legs. He knew the line of that waist. But, whoa — what was she doing here?

Carly's blue eyes bit into his as she slammed her hands onto her hips. "You."

He'd have said it at exactly the same time if it hadn't been for the big guy who lifted him clear off the floor and gripped him by the throat. He couldn't get a damned sound out. Not even a squeak.

Carly looked him up and down and narrowed her eyes, taking in his split lip and his dusty jeans.

"This is how you turn over a new leaf?"

Chapter Six

Carly stood as still as a statue, because it was either that or wobble on her feet. The man she'd barely pried herself away from that morning — the one she'd all but run away from because he was so terrifyingly hard to resist — had come to Twin Moon Ranch?

He's here! He's here! Her wolf jumped up and down, wagging its tail.

Stupid beast. Hadn't it been listening to her lecture about not getting involved with a man?

Mine! her wolf cried. *Mate!*

Crap. Why hadn't Luke — smoking hot, one-night stand Luke — hit the road like he was supposed to? And why was her body on fire all over again?

"What are you doing here?" she demanded, hating the way her heart went pitter-patter.

She'd been pushing away memories of last night ever since she'd arrived on the ranch, but now all the heated, sensual images flooded back. She remembered Luke's reverent touch. His raw, pulsing power. The need that had swept over her when they'd touched.

She closed her eyes, but that just made the memories stronger. Luke knew just how to lick her to the edge of shattering pleasure — then ease her back so he could tease and torture her a little more. She'd never made love with such passion. Never needed a man that badly. And she'd never, ever been so close to shedding joyous tears.

I didn't want last night to end, her wolf cried.

Which was why she'd forced herself away. One minute longer wrapped in his arms and she might have forgotten her vow never to grow close to a man.

Is that why you took his jacket? her wolf asked.

The jacket was a trophy, not a souvenir, she insisted.

Sure. Keep telling yourself that.

A good thing she'd left the leather jacket draped over the handlebar of her bike. Her siblings would be all over her if they picked up Luke's scent. Even at twenty-seven years old, they treated her like the baby of the family. Ty, her oldest brother, was the bossiest of the bunch. Tina was more like a mother than a sister at times, and even Carly's fun-loving brother, Cody, gave her hell for fooling around with anyone at all. He and Ty would flip out and play their older-brother, alpha-wolf cards if they knew she'd spent the night with Luke.

Did we have to leave Luke without saying good-bye? her wolf complained.

She nodded firmly. Leaving quickly made everything easier. After all, they'd only shared one little night of fun. No more, no less.

But looking at him now, feeling her heart do flips all over again, she wasn't so sure.

His lip was bleeding and his shirt was covered in dust, but he still looked like a million bucks. Even with Ty looming nearby — Ty, exuding raw alpha power like Zeus about to throw a thunderbolt — Luke didn't blink an eye. He just stood there with eyes that sparkled and spat, saying nothing, accepting a guilty sentence before being charged.

Maybe he really meant it about turning over a new leaf, her wolf murmured, impressed.

"Wait a minute. You know this guy?" Cody asked, turning to her.

Her sister, Tina, had hurried into the room along with the others, and she stared, too.

Ty's laser gaze bored into Carly, and the whole room went quiet. Deadly quiet.

Carly folded her arms over her chest and tipped her chin up. "None of your business." A second ticked by, and she glared at Luke. If he'd been any closer, she would have grabbed him by the shirt and given him a good shake. "What the hell are you doing here? You said you were just passing through."

"You told me you were just visiting."

Well, yes. She had the right to visit her family. But who the hell had invited him?

"Whoa. Wait," Tina said. "You really know each other? How?"

Carly shut her mouth and glared at Luke. How would she answer that question? Barely? Biblically?

She expected Luke to show a flicker of apology. A little humility. But what did the bastard do?

He grinned. Grinned, damn it! Just a tiny, hidden flash of a grin, but she caught it, all right. And boy, did it make her blood boil. She had enough problems getting her family to accept that she was all grown up. The last thing she needed was a passing fling to show up at the ranch.

A passing fling, you got that? She glared some more.

He tipped his head one way then the other, as if to say, *Maybe. Maybe not.*

Footsteps scuffed at the entrance as Stef and a very angry Kyle appeared. The scent of wolf clung to his shoulders, and his hair was disheveled as if he'd only just shifted forms. What was going on?

Kyle jabbed a finger toward Luke. "How many men have you killed? How many have you turned?"

Luke pursed his lips. His eyes flashed, and Carly wondered if he was counting bodies in his head.

How many of them had it coming? her wolf growled, supporting Luke.

She shook her head. She barely knew Luke, but she knew he was no more a cold-blooded murderer than either of her brothers. They'd both killed in their time, but only in defense of their families.

Luke looked a decade older as he considered the question. "I honestly came here to thank Kyle."

Thank Kyle for what? she nearly asked, but Luke was already going on.

"I didn't come to stir up trouble." Luke looked from Kyle to Ty and Cody. Then his eyes swung to hers and sparked. *And I sure as hell didn't expect you here.*

He was glad, though. She could see that in his eyes, too. Glad and confused, just as she was.

"What's this about you and North Ridge pack?" Ty barked.

Carly sucked in a deep breath, as did most everyone in the room. Stefanie went white, and Kyle growled audibly.

Carly had heard the stories about North Ridge. How Greer, a brute of an alpha, had come to Arizona, demanding that Stefanie be given up to his pack. A pack Greer had ruled with an iron fist, keeping all privileges for himself — including the privilege of taking any woman he desired, anytime. Kyle and Stef had nearly died fighting off that monster, but in the end, they'd done it. They'd killed Greer. It was Kyle's right to take over the leadership of North Ridge pack, but he'd chosen to stay at Twin Moon.

Carly stood a little stiffer. Her father was up at North Ridge now, acting as temporary alpha until a suitable leader could be found to continue cleaning up Greer's messy legacy.

She looked at Luke. Was he really part of that awful pack?

Luke's face fell. "I was born at North Ridge. My whole family is there. What's left of it, anyway."

When he trailed off, she couldn't help but fill in the blanks. Who had he lost? When? How?

"Why did you leave?" Ty demanded.

Luke pursed his lips, making Carly's wolf wag its tail. *I love it when he does that.*

"I was forced to leave when I was a kid. When Greer just started abusing his power." His voice grew bitter and cold. Distant.

More blanks to fill in. Carly wondered what abuses had touched upon Luke's family.

No reason to trust Luke, she reminded herself. *No reason to feel sorry for him.*

But she couldn't help it. Yes, he'd come from a corrupt pack, but he'd left as a kid. And she knew how hard the life of an outcast could be. Female shifters usually stayed with their home packs or transferred from one to another without trouble. But many alphas followed the tradition of ejecting powerful young males before they could challenge the leader's supremacy — a practice that created packs of wandering outcasts. Some were rogues who caused trouble wherever they went. Others formed drifter packs that weren't nearly as violent or untrustworthy as rogues.

Was Luke a rogue or a drifter? She remembered the scars amidst his tattoos and wondered if it mattered. What would she have done if she'd had to hit the road at fourteen?

Let's not even think about that, her wolf decided. And for once, she agreed.

"So you joined a rogue pack?" Kyle hurled the words at Luke. "How many humans did you attack? How many did you turn?"

Luke pursed his lips before speaking. "I was trying to break up that brawl. I wasn't trying to hurt anyone."

"How many humans did you turn shifter?" Kyle demanded.

Luke let out a long, slow breath before answering. "None. None survived."

"I survived," Kyle spat back.

Stefanie put a hand on Kyle's arm. Carly knew that neither Stef nor Kyle had a choice about being turned shifter, and it had been an agonizing process for both. They'd found their peace on Twin Moon Ranch, but that wouldn't make them less wary of a man like Luke.

A man trying hard to make a new start. She saw the truth in his eyes. The regret. The determination. But he'd been living on the edge for so long. Could he really reform? Did she really want him to? He had that edgy power to him, that restless gaze.

That gentle touch, her wolf added in a dreamy voice.

Gentle wasn't what she'd call a typical rogue, that was for sure.

That's what I love about him. Her wolf nodded. *The contrasts. The inconsistencies.*

I don't love him, she reminded herself. *I can't.*

Yes, you can.

Luke looked at Kyle. "Like I said, I just wanted to thank the man who killed Greer Steton. I came to tell him I wish I'd done it myself. That's all." Luke put his hands up. "I didn't come to make trouble or to scare anyone, especially not a kid."

The words came out all ragged, and for a split second, Carly saw past the hardened man and down to the boy he must have once been. A boy on the run.

Then Luke blinked, and the man was back again. A man who wore pride on one sleeve and regret on the other.

Kyle scowled. Ty ran a hand over his chin. Tina tapped her fingers on her jeans.

Carly didn't trust herself to speak. Not with a thousand emotions running around her soul — like sorrow for that young boy or anger for the way the male-dominated shifter world ran.

He needs us. We can help him, her wolf pleaded.

She huffed quietly. Luke didn't want or need help. She had to watch out for herself, not for him, or she'd end up like her mother — a weak, needy woman who'd let herself be ruled by one powerful man after another. A woman who even seemed *relieved* to give up control.

Did Luke look like he wanted to steal our soul? her wolf demanded.

Carly remembered Luke caressing her face with a look of wonder after they'd bonded for the first time. Luke shifting sideways in the bed afterward, asking if she had enough space.

You were the one snuggling against him, the beast pointed out. *Claiming that space.*

Well, she'd had to, hadn't she? The second you gave a man an inch, he would take a yard.

Not all men are like that.

She scoffed, thinking of her mother's infatuation first with her father and then with Brad, the wolf she'd hooked up with after Carly's father became too overbearing to endure.

She narrowed her eyes on Luke. Sooner or later, he was bound to show his dark side, right?

"That's all I wanted," Luke said quietly, and he sounded so sure — until he looked at her. Then he didn't look sure at all.

Maybe he wants more, Carly's wolf purred.

Luke gave a weary sigh and looked at the door. "Okay, so this was a mistake. I'm sorry, all right? I'll just head back on my way."

"What's the hurry to get to North Ridge?" Ty asked, blocking the way.

"What's it to you?"

"Our father is the acting alpha, running North Ridge pack until it gets back on its feet," Ty growled.

Luke's jaw swung open, and a second later, he murmured, "Like I said, I don't want to make trouble. I just want to help."

"Right. Help," Kyle muttered from the side of the room.

"Help? Why?" Tina asked at the same time.

"I have to get to North Ridge before—" Luke started, then snapped his mouth shut as if he'd said too much.

"Before what?" Ty demanded.

Luke looked from one face to another until his eyes locked on Carly's. His jaw locked as if holding back a secret.

She tilted her head at him. Why did this feel like such a make-or-break moment? Why was her heart beating so fast?

"Before North Ridge is attacked," Luke said in a low, gritty voice.

The room went silent for a minute, then everyone spoke up at the same time.

"Attacked?"

"Who's planning to attack?"

Carly balled her hands into fists. Twin Moon pack had grown so powerful, they rarely feared intruders anymore. But North Ridge was vulnerable, and that was her father up there.

"I said, who's planning an attack?" Ty snarled.

Any other man would have trembled, but Luke leveled his gaze on Ty. His fingers scratched at his jeans, though, as if he was measuring how much to reveal.

The clock ticked in the silence that ensued, and suddenly, Carly understood. If Luke was serious about a fresh start, his best chance to win her father's trust lay in warning him of the impending attack. If Luke told Ty, however, he relinquished that ace — and with it, his best chance to be accepted at North Ridge.

A selfish man, she figured, would guard the information with his life or sell it at a high price. A good man, on the other hand, would share the knowledge so that the families at North Ridge could be safe.

Carly stared at Luke, holding her breath.

He hesitated one second longer, then spoke quietly. "A rogue named Steen van Kleij."

There, his stony expression said. *I did it. I did the right thing, even though I just screwed myself.*

Carly let out the breath she'd been holding.

"Steen van who?" Cody asked.

"Steen van Kleij," Carly said, ignoring her brothers' stares. Of course she knew the name. "Second-in-command to one of the more notorious rogue gangs that cruise the West Coast." The kind Arroyo Hills pack made sure to guard against.

"How many? When? Where?" Ty demanded, looking ready to barrel out the door and hunt them down.

"Wait. How do you know this?" Cody asked, and all eyes jumped to Luke again.

His eyes flickered to Carly's, and she gulped. Her brothers were good, fair men, but they'd stop at nothing to protect family and friends. Did Luke know how dangerous a position he was in? And whoa, why had he even come to Twin Moon Ranch?

To do the right thing, her wolf whispered. *To start again.*

Luke took a deep breath, then looked at Ty again. "Let's just say I've had some run-ins with Steen's gang. A week ago, I got word they were looking to take over a pack of their own."

A little like Craig, Carly thought in disgust. Men who looked for the easy way to the top. Except that Craig came from a privileged family, unlike the rogues.

"A rogue pack is planning to take over North Ridge?" Cody scowled.

Luke's eyes flashed, making it clear he was as enraged as anyone else. "Not if I can help it."

Ty scowled and corrected him. "Not if I can help it." He looked to Tina, who nodded back. "We'll let Dad know and send a team of our best men to help him repel any attack."

Luke closed his eyes, and Carly's heart ached for him. Had he just given away his best hope of rejoining North Ridge pack? Of settling down and living a normal life?

Carly caught Tina studying Luke, too, as if she understood what he'd just done.

"Tell me again why you left North Ridge," Tina said.

Carly glared at her sister. Hadn't Luke already explained? Why was Tina pushing him so much?

Because some men aren't very good at voicing what needs to be said, her sister told her in a private aside.

Luke's face went rock hard. His hands clenched at his sides, and it was a long time before he spoke. When he did, it was in a low, hushed voice.

"It started with just the single women. He'd butter them up and play with one after another."

The words took a minute to click in Carly's mind. Luke meant Greer. That awful Greer.

"But it went from games with single women to not-games with women who didn't want him. Greer didn't give them a choice, and he was too powerful to stop. Too powerful for anyone to intervene when he started on the mated women and the younger girls. Anyone he decided he wanted. Anytime."

Carly cringed, imagining life under an alpha like that.

His look became a glare, but it wasn't aimed at anyone in the room. It was unfocused, targeted at something in the past.

"My father tried to stop Greer. I wanted to help him, but my mother wouldn't let me. I was fourteen. Fucking fourteen. What could I do?"

Carly's wolf whimpered, and it took everything she had to resist the urge to reach out and touch him.

"My father challenged Greer the honorable way — one-on-one, but Greer called out all his men and outnumbered my dad and the others. Of course, Greer didn't have them killed outright. They were strung up, one by one, as an example to everyone else."

She gulped.

"We had to watch them kick and gasp and. . ." Luke trailed off, but his nails made scratching noises against his jeans.

She felt sick, just imagining the scene.

Luke opened his mouth then closed it again, giving her the impression he was leaving something out. Then his jaw hardened. "My mother brought me to the edge of pack territory and told me to run and run and never look back. So I did."

It was hard picturing Luke as a kid — and even harder to picture him running away from trouble instead of charging straight into it. But the hard edge in his voice spoke of trials and tribulations. He rubbed a scar on his hand absently and clenched his hands into tight fists.

The council house went quiet as everyone processed his words. Even Kyle, who'd had a rough childhood, didn't glare quite as ferociously any more.

Finally, Ty snapped his fingers, signaling for two lower-ranking wolves to escort Luke out of the council house. Luke followed them after a quick glance in her direction.

A glance that said, *I wish. . .*

Carly held her breath, wrestling back her own wishes.

"Get moving," the wolf at Luke's side grunted, pushing him toward the door.

Carly's wolf whimpered, seeing him go.

"So what do we do?" Tina asked when the door closed.

"We send the guy packing," Ty growled.

Carly's wolf whimpered.

"He could make trouble for North Ridge," Kyle pointed out.

"Maybe not," Cody said. "Maybe he means what he says."

Ty ground his teeth. "Are we really going to trust this guy? This rogue?"

"I'm not saying we trust him," Cody replied. "I'm saying we let him prove himself."

Carly felt her hopes swell, which was crazy, because she didn't need to take Luke's side, right?

"Maybe Cody's right. Maybe we should give him a chance," Tina said.

Ty folded his arms. "How?"

Everyone seemed at a loss for words, until one voice spoke up.

"Keep him here a while. Put him to work. Hard work."

Carly blinked, because whoa — was that her doing the suggesting? The last thing she wanted was for Luke to stay. One-night stands were supposed to disappear, not stick around. But, damn. Her sneaky wolf had gotten the words past the conscious part of her mind.

"Not a bad idea," Tina said.

Wait, Carly wanted to blurt. *It's a terrible idea!* But it was too late.

"That way, we can judge if he's really willing to help," Tina continued. "We can see whether Dad can trust him at North Ridge."

Of course he can't be trusted, Carly wanted to say. He was a man.

"Dad has had enough problems getting that pack back on its feet," Cody added. "Maybe this guy can actually help."

Carly scratched her head. Her father had invited her to North Ridge several times. Maybe he needed more help than his pride allowed him to admit. Maybe he really could use someone like Luke.

Dad can use us, too, her wolf murmured.

Tina had encouraged Carly to join their father at North Ridge, too. *God knows the women of that pack have been through hell. What they need is a few strong women to help them balance things out. Women like you.*

She'd been tempted, for sure. At North Ridge, she could make a difference to a pack's future the way she never could in her California pack or at Twin Moon Ranch.

But, shit. If Luke was headed to Colorado, she sure as hell couldn't go.

"We're really going to let this guy stay?" Kyle protested. "Right here among our families? What if he's lying?"

"Don't worry," Cody said. "We'll keep a close eye on him. And just think. We can use an extra hand with some of the projects no one's excited about taking on."

"Like what?" Tina asked.

Cody flashed a sly smile. "Oh, I have a few ideas. What do you think, Ty?"

Ty looked like he'd prefer getting rid of Luke the old-fashioned way, but when Lana put a hand on his arm, he took a deep breath and nodded.

"You set it up. And keep a good eye on him."

"You bet I will," Cody said. "Any volunteers to help?"

"Me," Kyle grunted. "Believe me, I'll keep an eye on him."

Me, too! Me, too! Carly's wolf cried, but she batted it down. No way was she admitting what she felt for this man to anyone.

Not even herself.

Chapter Seven

Four days later...

Luke had survived a lot of bad times. Desperate times, when he hadn't known where to go. Hungry times, when he was young and struggling to hang on. Rough-and-tumble times, as he'd fought his way to the top of the drifter pack.

But he'd never experienced anything like the last four days.

Four bone-aching days in which the wolves of Twin Moon Ranch had thrown everything at him they could. One break-your-will test after another.

"You want to prove yourself, wolf?" the alpha, Ty Hawthorne, had challenged him. "Do it. Starting right there."

Right there was the old cesspit beside Kyle Williams' house. The place had once been a bunkhouse with no amenities except an outhouse. The cesspit had been covered over ages ago, but the rotten boards were threatening to cave in. The pit needed to be mucked out, filled in, and covered over so the area was secure for kids.

Kids who seemed to have been evacuated for the time it took Luke to finish that miserable job, because Kyle Williams didn't trust him one bit. The guy watched Luke like a hawk the whole time — whether Luke was up to his knees in petrified shit, tossing shovel after shovel up or hauling it away in a wheelbarrow. It was nowhere near as messy as he'd feared — in fact, the setting in the shade of mighty cottonwoods might even be called nice. But the work was backbreaking, and the symbolism burned his soul. The wolves of Twin Moon Ranch hadn't just forced him to his knees — they'd put him a level lower than any living creature on earth.

It would have been easier if Kyle had jeered or shown sick satisfaction in seeing Luke forced to stoop so low, but he didn't. He just looked on with grim distrust, reminding Luke how much proving he really had to do.

So, no — Kyle didn't say much, and Luke worked in quiet monotony. The others would come and go, checking on his work. Ty would stop by and glower. The pack's main tracker, Zack, would pause, have a word with Kyle, and shoot Luke glares of warning.

Make sure you never mess with my pack, asshole. Don't you dare mess with us.

Luke gritted his teeth and worked on. Each of those men was a powerful alpha type, though Ty was obviously the top dog. Still, Luke's inner wolf itched to take them on. He figured he stood a fair chance, too, but that wasn't the point. He had a new type of battle to fight now — an inner battle that was all about holding back instead of lashing out.

And, shit. Who'd have thought showing no reaction would be so hard?

He stripped to the waist and sweated buckets under the searing sun. It wasn't summer, but boy, did the desert heat up. Every fly on the ranch seemed to give up on the livestock in their rush to get over to him. They buzzed around his head and tried landing on his lips.

Luke cursed under his breath as he worked. Not only had he messed up his chance to beat Steen van Kleij to North Ridge and be welcomed as a hero by delivering the news of the rogues — now he was a goddamned slave to the wolves of Twin Moon Ranch.

"You miserable yet?" Cody asked cheerfully. It was his turn to keep an eye on Luke, though Kyle was lurking somewhere nearby, too.

Luke nearly snarled *yes* in reply. But deep down, the answer was no. He wasn't miserable. Tired, yes. Sore, absolutely. And thirstier than he'd ever been before. But in spite of it all, it felt good, in a way. Like he was doing penance for his sins. Cleansing his soul. Proving himself, one shovelful at a time.

"Not yet," he murmured, pushing the shovel deeper with his foot.

"Maybe we ought to work you harder." Cody laughed in another one of his impossible-to-interpret moments. Was Cody goading him, or was he genuinely an upbeat guy?

"Maybe," Luke murmured, refusing to take the bait.

It had taken him a while to puzzle out who was who on this ranch, but he'd finally figured it out. Cody — the most relaxed, easygoing wolf shifter Luke had ever met — was Carly's full brother. The pack's thundercloud of an alpha, Ty, was Carly's half-brother. Same father, different mothers, apparently. Tina, the dark-haired she-wolf, was another half-sibling. But no one here seemed to do anything by halves. They all seemed equally close.

The whole ranch was like that, in fact. One big, happy family in which everyone was ready to drop everything to cover each other's backs. In a word, a pack. A very tight-knit pack. Kyle, the cop he'd mauled all those years ago, had been human, yet even he had become part of this extended family together with his mate.

They were all on the inside, while Luke was on the outside. Way, way outside.

He wiped the sweat off his brow and tossed another shovel upward, resisting the urge to throw it at Cody.

Cody laughed as if he'd imagined the same thing, then grew more serious. "You can take a water break, you know."

Luke squinted up at him. So Cody was genuinely a decent guy, it seemed. And though a short break didn't sound bad, Luke shook his head. He didn't need water. He needed to prove something to the wolves of Twin Moon Ranch — and to himself.

Cody stretched and walked away. "Do as you please. I'll be right back. Time for a changing of the guard."

That happened several times a day — a different wolf coming by to keep an eye on him — so when yet another pair of boots paraded by at eye level in the heat of the afternoon, Luke barely looked up. Until he realized the boots came with pretty laces and a pair of swinging tassels.

Carly. His breath caught before he even looked up. And when he looked up—

His heart skipped and hopped, and what was sure to be a goofy grin spread across his face. He forgot about the blisters on his hands and the long list of jobs that stretched out ahead of him. All he saw was her.

Mate! Mine! His wolf did a happy dance.

A happy dance in a cesspool. He was definitely nuts.

Carly's legs were a mile long, especially from that angle. Her hair shone like fool's gold, which was fitting, given the way his mind switched off. Her tank top hugged her curves, and his fingers twitched, remembering the way she'd heated under his touch.

"I warned you, didn't I?" she said, squatting down.

He wiped his brow. "Warned me of what?"

"Turning over a new leaf isn't worth it. Look at you. You're wallowing in lonely misery."

He laughed, and damn, did it feel good. So good, it was pretty much the highlight of his day. But then again, that wouldn't be hard.

Carly's gaze strayed over his bare, sweaty chest before she yanked it back to his face, and his mind flashed back to their night together. Clearly, she hadn't purged the memories either, no matter how she pretended not to care. So, yeah. That was definitely the highlight of his day. His week. His month. Hell, maybe even his whole year.

She's the highlight of my life, his wolf whispered.

"Wallowing? I guess I am. Miserable? A little," he admitted. "But lonely? No. Not any more."

He locked his eyes on hers and took a deep breath, inhaling her sweet scent.

Sparks bubbled in Carly's eyes. Her lower lip trembled a tiny little bit, telling him he wasn't the only one wishing for another night. Maybe even more than one night. Maybe even—

He scowled and looked at his boots. Sure. Right. She was a member of the pack's ruling family, and he was... standing in a pit of petrified shit.

Carly motioned around. "Are you saying this is worth it?"

It wasn't a tease this time. Her breath caught as she awaited his answer, as if she really, really had to know. As if she was considering reinventing herself, too.

"Seriously," she said. "Is it worth it?"

He contemplated the edge of his shovel. He could escape this ranch in a heartbeat if he set his mind to it. And yet, he hadn't done that. Instead, he was up to his waist in muck and planning the long road ahead. Was it worth it?

He nodded slowly. "Yeah. It is."

She cocked her head, looking for some sign of a lie. Her lips pursed, and she grew serious, even contemplative. A different Carly. A quieter, more earnest one.

His wolf hummed inside, and the whole desert seemed to lean closer, listening in. A fresh breeze tickled the air with the scent of flowers, making it feel as if he'd taken Carly's hand and walked her to the shade of a cool stream. The earth heated, and his cheeks flushed. Hers, too.

Kiss her, the desert whispered. *Kiss your mate.*

He ran his tongue over his cracked lips. When another whisper reached into his mind, he clutched the shovel harder.

Kiss him. Was that Carly's wolf, urging her on?

The blue of her eyes was brighter than ever when her gaze dropped to his lips. She leaned closer, and he did, too, holding his breath. Waiting. Wishing. Dreaming. The kind of dream that had been getting him through the roughest moments of the past few days.

A dream of Carly Daredevil Hawthorne, kissing him.

He could picture it so easily. He'd rock to the balls of his feet and let his lips close over hers to savor the taste of the world's most delicious she-wolf. Her silky hair would cascade over his hands, and the sun would illuminate it in a heavenly glow. Her body would heat against his, and she'd slide closer, inviting him to touch and explore.

Just one kiss, his wolf begged. *Just one.*

Her eyes went a little glassy, asking for the same thing. *I need you like you need me.*

Which was crazy. What would a woman like Carly need from a man like him?

The breeze wafted through the cottonwoods, making the leaves dance, and the whisper worked its way to his soul. *Peace.* The sound carried like the voice of a wise old man. *She needs peace.*

He pondered that one. Wasn't he the one with an ugly past to come to terms with?

Kiss her, the desert said. Or maybe that wasn't the desert. Maybe it was destiny.

Kiss me, her quivering lip agreed.

Carly rocked forward at exactly the same time that he did, and their lips brushed. But then a horse whinnied in the distance, and Carly broke away, blinking wildly.

Luke sucked in a deep breath. Whoa. What had he been thinking?

Footsteps sounded, not too far away, and a big man — the local blacksmith, a boar shifter — waved to Carly and continued on his way.

She cleared her throat and tossed her hair, pulling herself together far more quickly than Luke did.

"Well, keep at it, then, Hot Stuff," she said, morphing from needy she-wolf to brassy, confident Carly with every word. "Keep at it."

When she walked away, his eyes trailed after her. Part of his soul did, too, dragging along like a puppy who didn't want to be left behind.

You can't change who you really are, deep down inside, she'd said to him in the bar, in a way that suggested she'd tried for herself.

He wondered how hard she'd tried and why. Wondered who she was inside.

The shirt she wore was emblazoned with a bungee jumping logo — another clue in the riddle that was Carly. What was she out to prove, taking all those risks? That she was invincible? Was she trying to punish someone — and if so, whom? Herself or her loved ones?

His wolf perked up at the thought. *Loved ones. If I love her...*

He shook the thought away and ordered himself back to work. One shovelful, then another. A third.

No more dreaming, he told his wolf with every heave.

But when he heard Carly's step again, he turned around eagerly.

"Hi, Car—"

The smile froze on his face because it wasn't Carly, after all. It was whatshername — Audrey — the she-wolf who'd ferreted him out on his first day and refused to leave him alone.

"Luke. Honey," she purred in a voice that dripped saccharine as she leaned over to greet him. So far over, her low-cut top left nothing to the imagination.

"Hi," he said, averting his eyes.

If he were still a horny teenager, the sight of her fleshy tits tussling with each other under that thin top might have turned him on, but not any more. If anything, the sight had the opposite effect.

"How's it going, sugar?" she cooed.

It had been going a hell of a lot better a few minutes ago.

"Fine, I guess." He couldn't throw a shovel full of dirt up with her right there, so he transferred it from the left corner of the pit to the right. Anything to keep his eyes off what he really didn't want to see.

Audrey wore her hair in a big, poofy style, bleached so often all the life had gone out of it. She leaned so far over, he was afraid she'd stage a fall and launch herself right into his arms. As it was, he was amazed Audrey didn't keel over from the weight of the long, fake eyelashes she kept batting at him.

"I run a styling salon, you know," she whispered seductively.

Luke blinked, wondering if she had a room in the back for "entertaining" certain customers. The second Audrey had found him on the ranch, she'd introduced herself and offered him a free cut and shave — a very close shave, as she'd put it. Her eyes had danced over his body.

A cut, he didn't need. A shave, yes, but not by her. No way.

"And I was thinking—" she started.

"Audrey!" Cody yelled, giving Luke the evil eye. As if Luke was the one cornering Audrey and not the other way around.

Audrey straightened quickly, but the gleam didn't go out of her eye. It just shifted over to Cody.

"Why, hello, cowboy." She faced Cody with a deft wiggle that made the right sleeve of her shirt slip off her shoulder. "What can I do for you?"

She licked her lips, communicating a dozen options to Cody, who pursed his lips and jabbed a thumb over his shoulder.

"Um... Ty wants to see you."

Luke arched his left eyebrow. He'd bet a hundred bucks Ty didn't want to see any more of Audrey than he had to.

But, hell, it worked, because Audrey's eyes sparkled and she immediately strutted off. "Bye-bye, boys. Bye-bye."

Luke leaned on his shovel and watched her go with a sick kind of fascination. Were women like her real?

You ought to know, his wolf grumbled. *You fooled around with a few in your time.*

That was before I found my mate— he started, then stopped himself a little too late.

Told you. His wolf grinned. *Told you Carly is our mate.*

Cody sighed and turned to Luke, offering a hand to pull him out of the pit.

"Quick break."

It was more order than offer, and Cody underscored it by throwing a heavy arm over Luke's shoulders the second he was upright. He steered Luke to a tree stump where a water bottle stood in the shade.

"You might have figured out what Audrey is interested in," Cody said.

Luke figured a nod wasn't required.

"But Carly..." Cody trailed off, fishing for words. "In case you didn't know, she's my baby sister." Cody jerked a thumb in the direction Carly had gone.

She's my mate, Luke's wolf growled quietly.

Cody went on as casually as if talking about the weather or the crops.

"I'm not sure why she keeps stopping around here..."

Luke's wolf growled. *Because deep down, she knows we're mates, too.*

"...but if you touch my baby sister, I will rip you limb from limb." Cody flashed a broad grin that said, *Yes, I am a nice guy. And no, I am not kidding. I will happily rip you limb from limb.*

Luke studied Cody, sizing him up as his wolf urged him to respond to that challenge with his own.

We can take this guy. We can fight any wolf in this pack. We can earn our mate!

He took a deep breath, fighting back the urge to act. He wasn't here to challenge the local wolves or fight for a girl. He was here to prove himself. Could he really clean up his act? Was there any good left under all the bad?

He gulped enough water to drown a camel, hoping to wash thoughts of Carly away, and went back to work. Well, he tried to, anyway. But every shovelful of dirt, every drop of sweat that poured down his face only seemed to reinforce the image of her in his mind. And no matter what he did, the dry wind teased him with her scent.

Mate, the desert whispered insistently. *Get out there and win her before...*

He stopped abruptly and sniffed the wind. Before what?

Dark images swirled through his mind, all blurry and monochrome. Was there trouble afoot? Was Carly in danger?

Before what? He wanted to hiss back as he eyed the clouds over the hills.

Before it's too late, the wind whispered. *Before it's too late.*

Chapter Eight

"How's it going, sweetheart?" a shrill voice cackled over Carly's phone.

Carly took a deep breath, telling herself to be patient. "Fine, Mom. How are you?"

"Oh, fine, sweetie. Do you have a minute to talk?"

"I have a minute." She checked her watch. "I promised the kids I'd go for a walk with them. I'm just about to pick them up."

She was just about to kill Audrey, too, after seeing the hairdresser saunter over to Luke with lust in her eyes. The thought made her nauseous. That was Carly's man, not Audrey's.

But, oops. He wasn't her man. She didn't want him, right?

Wrong, her wolf sulked.

"So, how was the drive to Arizona?" her mother asked.

"Fine," Carly said, letting her gaze stray over the ranch. The sky went on forever, just like the pastures seemed to. Copper bells hung around the necks of the sheep clanged at intervals as the flock rooted through the scrub. It was all so timeless. So peaceful. So harsh yet so fragile.

A little like your heart, her wolf murmured.

She ignored it and forced on a cheery tone. "The trip was fine. Easy. No problem."

Okay, so that wasn't entirely true. She left out the part about the SUV that had nearly run her off the road by Indio. She also left out that eerie feeling of having been followed all the way from Palm Springs to the Arizona border. She hadn't been driving as fast as usual on that stretch of highway because the cops were out in droves, and some sixth sense had her looking over her shoulder every few seconds. She'd only shaken the feeling when she opened up the throttle at the Arizona border.

She scowled. She'd been so obsessed with Luke lately that she'd pushed that episode completely out of her mind. Maybe she'd been imagining things. Anyway, she was on the ranch now, so it didn't matter, right?

"Did you get in before dark?" her mother asked.

"Um, I stopped for the night," Carly said. The cleaned-up version of *I stopped for a wild night of screwing a wolf I barely know, and now I can't get him out of my mind.*

"Thank goodness," her mother said. "It's so much safer than driving through the night."

Carly kept her lips sealed. If only her mother knew.

"How's everyone?"

"Everyone is doing just fine," Carly sighed as she walked up to Ty's house. Her brother was sitting on the patio, holding an impossibly tiny bundle on his shoulder. Both of them looked firmly asleep.

"Hi, Ty," she called.

Ty's right eye cracked open with a look that said, *If you wake this child, I will kill you.*

She covered the phone with her hand, coming closer. "Get much sleep last night?"

Ty shifted slightly so she could see a tiny little nose and two dark splashes of eyes.

Her heart skipped a beat, and something in her soul moved. The child was that gorgeous. That much of a miracle. That amazing—

She cleared her throat and leaned away before her wolf got carried away.

"I've forgotten what sleep is," Ty grumbled, though his lips quirked at the same time and a massive hand stroked the tiny back with a soft touch she'd never have thought her brother capable of.

Her siblings were all in baby heaven — even though they liked to pretend it was hell. Little Tyson was Ty and Lana's third. Meanwhile, her older sister, Tina, was pregnant, and Cody doted on his daughters so much, it seemed only a matter of time before he and Heather had another. They all loved joking that Carly would be the next to take a mate.

As if.

"Is Tana ready to go?" Carly asked.

Soon, Ty said, shooting the words into her mind so as not to disturb the baby.

"How's your father?" her mother's voice rose, pulling Carly back to the phone.

She made a face and moved off a short distance. She could hear the wistfulness in her mother's words. All the crushed hopes of a love that had blossomed then crashed and burned decades ago. Would her mother ever get over her first love?

"Dad's not here. He's in Colorado, remember?"

"Oh, now I remember," her mother said. Which was about as truthful as Carly saying her trip was fine. Her mother had lost part of her mind when Carly's father rejected her, despite the fact that he was a powerful, self-centered alpha who didn't know the meaning of love.

And you do? her wolf snorted.

Sure, she did. She loved her mother, regardless of how batty the woman was. She loved her siblings. She'd even fallen in love with a few men in her time, too. It was just that she fell back out of love.

Not with Luke, her wolf insisted. *He's the one.*

"Craig was asking about you," her mother went on.

Carly made a face and crinkled her nose. Craig wasn't the first unwanted suitor she'd had, and he probably wouldn't be the last. But he was so damned persistent. Persistent and powerful — a bad combination.

We ought to get him together with Audrey, her wolf grumbled. *That tramp.*

"Brad says Craig is perfect for you." Her mother's voice rose in glee.

"What do you think?" Carly shot back. Not that she wanted her mother's opinion. She just wanted the woman to think for herself instead of parroting her mate.

"Well, Brad is usually right."

Carly rolled her eyes. "Well, tell Brad I'm not interested in Craig. Tell Craig I'm not interested, either. Oh, wait. I already told both of them to their faces, didn't I?"

Carly caught her voice rising and forced herself to slow down. Okay, so her mother was weak and dependent. The important thing was not to become like that herself. To stay strong. To avoid men like Craig and Luke and live her own life.

Luke is nothing like Craig, her wolf snarled.

"I just think you ought to consider settling down, honey."

"With Craig? Never."

Her mother let out a loud, martyred sigh. "Well, he's gone now, anyway. I hope you won't regret missing your chance."

Alarm bells went off in her mind. The leading alpha of Arroyo Hills had offered Craig a job — one with a clear path to eventual pack leadership if Craig was willing to put in the years of hard work as a worthy alpha would.

Obviously, Craig was looking for a faster track to the top. An easier way. But where?

"Where did Craig go?"

Her mother made a vague sound. "He said something about hooking up with some friends and checking out a new pack to lead. That man's moving up in the world, I tell you."

Carly's mind spun. "New pack? What new pack?"

She'd seen the greed in Craig's eyes the last time they'd met. He wasn't a man on the lookout for a pack to serve — he wanted a pack to lord over, just like he'd wanted to lord over her. And young bucks didn't exactly get voted into power — not in the shifter world. If Craig had turned down the offer at Arroyo Hills, he was probably plotting to overthrow an alpha somewhere. Some packs were ruled by family dynasties, like Twin Moon Ranch. Others saw leaders come and go in a series of violent takeovers — including packs like North Ridge.

"He didn't mention." Her mother's voice was so vague and disinterested, Carly wanted to scream.

What if Craig had his eye on North Ridge? And, shit. Maybe that was the root of Craig's quest to take her as his mate. He certainly hadn't shown genuine interest in her when he'd turned up out of the blue.

Not like Luke, her wolf whispered.

And there it was again — the memory of Luke brushing a finger over her eyebrow then tucking her hair behind her ear. When he'd lain face-to-face with her after they'd made love, his eyes had sparked with wonder, just as they had when she visited him before walking to Ty's house.

Not lonely, he'd said. *Not any more.*

She closed her eyes, trying desperately to keep her armor in place.

"I really think he could be the one for you," her mother said. She meant Craig, of course, but all Carly saw was an image of Luke, looking deep into her eyes.

"Carly! Carly!"

Little Tana and her cousin, Holly, skipped up, as bright and sunny as the Arizona sky on a warm summer's night. But it wasn't summer, and Carly sensed ominous clouds looming somewhere beyond the horizon. She'd witnessed storms sweep over the ranch in a matter of minutes to batter the buildings with rain, hail, and wind. The desert could be like that, springing surprises from out of the blue.

"I have to go, Mom," Carly murmured.

"Have fun, sweetheart. Kiss your father for me."

"I told you—" Carly started, then gave up. "Okay, Mom. Thanks for calling. Bye."

"Hi! Hi!" the girls cried, hugging her legs.

Carly did her best to settle her emotions as she hugged them back. There was nothing to worry about. North Ridge pack had been warned to keep their guard up. And anyway, Craig was no match for her father, regardless of the age difference. Craig would have to assemble a solid group of powerful supporters to pose a genuine threat.

So, really, there was nothing to worry about. Everything would be okay. Carly tucked her phone into her pocket and smiled at the kids.

"Hi, girls. Ready to go?"

"Ready!" Tana declared.

"Can we feed the horses?" Holly begged.

Carly nodded, trying to snap her focus to the kids.

"We've been stuck at home all day," Tana complained.

Normally, her nieces had the run of the ranch, but with Luke around, their parents had kept the kids close to home. Well, Carly knew about needing the freedom to roam.

"Sure. Let's go feed the horses."

"Yay! Let's go!" Tana cried.

The kids grabbed her hands and hurried her up the hill, where the horses nickered in greeting.

"Look! Missy had a baby." Holly pointed at the palomino in the second pasture.

"My mommy had a baby, too," Tana said.

Carly smiled. Yeah, that was one of the reasons for her visit — to meet her new nephew, Ty and Lana's third child. Their third! She shook her head, wondering what had gotten into her brother and his sensible mate. Kids were lots of fun, but taking care of three of them? All the time?

I think that would be nice, her wolf chipped in.

"Aunt Tina and Uncle Rick are having a baby soon, too," Holly said.

Carly sighed. Friday nights were duller than ever on the ranch. It was funny how she always counted down the days to her next visit to the ranch, then counted down the time until she could leave again. To some undefined place she could get a fresh start in and call her own.

"So you two will get another cousin soon," she said as they walked.

"How soon? Tomorrow?" Tana tried.

"On my birthday!" Holly clapped. "Aunt Tina could have a baby on my birthday!"

Carly laughed. Holly's birthday was two weeks away, and Tina was still in her first trimester.

"Sweetie, it takes nine months to make a baby."

"Why? How?"

Carly kept her lips sealed. No way was she going to explain sex to a couple of curious preschoolers.

And, whoa. Just the thought of sex made her mind slide straight over to that incredible night with Luke.

I didn't want that night to end, her wolf whimpered.

Which was why she'd had to leave so quickly the morning after and why she'd been avoiding him — or trying to force herself to — over the past few days.

The problem was, she'd been thinking of him day and night. Moping. Wishing. Thirsting for more. And the scary thing was, she wasn't just daydreaming about the sex. She was thinking about watching him sleep or smiling that out-of-the-blue smile.

"Are you going to have a baby, Carly?" Tana asked.

She choked so violently, the nearest horses skittered away. "Um, I doubt it."

"Why not?"

"Because she needs a mate first," Holly told Tana.

Carly snorted. "Not getting mated, believe me. Never. And don't let anyone tell you you have to, either."

"Daddy says I never have to get a mate," Tana agreed.

That, Carly could picture. Her brother, the big bad alpha, was already stressed about the thought of his little girl growing up. Ha. She couldn't wait to see him dealing with his stubborn daughter *then.*

"Why not? Holly asked. "Mommy says she loves Daddy. And Daddy loves her."

Carly waved her hand vaguely. It was hard to explain to someone who assumed the whole world had stable and loving parents. "Well, if you find the person you love, then it's great. It's just not for everyone."

Keep kidding yourself, her wolf snorted.

"Daddy says I can get a dog when I'm grown up," Tana announced.

Carly smiled. Ty was right. Dogs loved you unconditionally. Dogs didn't play power games the way men did.

"So will you get a dog, Carly?" Holly persisted.

Just Luke, her wolf replied. *All I want is my mate.*

Don't have a mate. Don't need a mate.

Carly repeated the mantra through the next half hour of feeding horses, then looked up at the bluffs, her favorite place to get away from it all while she was on the ranch. "Let's go explore the mesa."

They came across Stef and little Keith on the way, and soon, they were a merry band of five.

"Yay! Rock-climbing!" Tana squeaked, pulling her on.

"Sounds good," Stef said. "I haven't been climbing in a while."

See? Carly told her wolf. *The minute you mate and have kids, it's all over.*

Her wolf snorted. *Didn't we see Stef zip by on her mountain bike yesterday?*

Okay, okay, so Stef seemed to be living the best of both worlds, with a loving mate, a job she loved, a son she adored, and plenty of adventures to pursue.

So what are you afraid of? Carly's wolf cried.

Afraid? She wasn't afraid of anything. Except maybe losing her heart.

"Here's the spot," Carly said, hushing the beast within while she looked up from the base of the mesa. Orange-toned rock undulated in waves, serrated by a series of cracks that provided just enough handholds to make things interesting.

"Carly is an expert rock-climber," Tana told Stef.

"So I've heard." Stef winked at her.

"She even works at a rock-climbing store," Tana went on.

Carly stifled a laugh. She worked part-time at an outdoor outfitter's outlet, but her real job was all the unpaid work she did for her home pack. All the women who didn't have the nerve to approach the alpha came to her to voice their concerns, and she constantly found herself lobbying for one thing or another on their behalf. More childcare. A better community center. More funding for interpack projects to keep rogues at bay. Of course, all that was hard to explain to Tana, who focused on the rock-climbing part.

"Have you been recruited to chaperone the field trip yet?" Stef asked as they threw down their backpacks and let the kids drink.

Carly nodded. Every year the school kids went on a field trip where they piled into a covered wagon and recreated pioneer days.

"Wouldn't miss it," she murmured truthfully. As a kid, she'd always missed the event, just as she had missed out on so many other things by living with her mom.

"Yay! I can't wait!" Holly skipped and jumped.

Carly tousled her niece's hair. "Me neither. Now, go at that rock. Show me what you can do."

"Just bouldering," Stef told the kids. "Don't go too high."

The kids kept to the lowest level — low enough that they could hop to the ground if they lost their grip. Stef and Carly did, too.

Well, Carly did for a while. But eventually, she found herself climbing higher. She couldn't help it. Instinct drew her to cracks and overhangs that provided more challenge. To the kinds of views that made her feel like a soaring eagle and not a mere dweller of the earth. To heights that reminded her of her most epic ascents.

"You're a little high, aren't you?" Stef called from below.

Carly eyed the forty-foot drop and shrugged. "Eh. It's not that high."

Stef looked around and called in a whisper-shout. "Seriously, what if you fell?"

Carly sighed. Stef sounded like Tina. Or worse, like the older ranch ladies who scolded her all the time.

Do you have to go so high?

Do you have to drive so fast?

Do you have a death wish or what?

She didn't have a death wish. She had a lust for life.

You'll kill me with worry, her mother would say, clutching her heart.

You'll kill yourself someday, Tina had once said, grabbing her arms in a sisterly heart-to-heart. *Promise you won't ever make me go through that. Promise you'll be careful.*

She was careful. Well, careful enough. What were they all so worried about?

"The good thing about being a shifter," she called down with a grunt, "is that we heal fast."

"Heal? From a fall from that high?" Stef sounded skeptical.

"This is nothing," Carly shot back. Her voice was cavalier, but an out-of-nowhere memory made her wince. She'd taken a bad fall two years ago in the Sierras and, yes, it had hurt. Murderously. But she'd patched up perfectly well, right?

Her wolf whimpered and stuck its tail between its legs, remembering another close call. That terrifying moment on Half Dome in Yosemite National Park. She'd free-climbed the whole damn thing in a stunt that had the rock-climbing world buzzing. A good thing no one had seen her bobble near the top. She'd slipped and scraped her nails to a bloody mess before two fingers miraculously caught on a tiny ledge. She'd hung there by one hand, looking down at the longest fall of her life, her heart beating in triple time as the seconds ticked past.

But she'd gotten her shit together and continued to the top. Triumph had chased the fear away, and she'd grinned for weeks afterward. She was practically immune to death, it seemed. She was strong and capable, and even if she bobbled, her body could take any injury, any time, any place.

Right?

Can't we slow down a little? Stop and smell the roses? her wolf begged.

Carly ignored it, climbing higher until it was just her, the desert breeze, and miles of open space. She climbed on and on, then hauled herself over a ledge and stood panting at the top.

Her special place. A place where the earth fell away from the sheer cliff she'd just ascended and the desert stretched to a horizon so distant, she couldn't pinpoint the border between earth and sky. The perfect place to clear her mind. Up here, she could stand tall, independent, and free.

Alone, her wolf whimpered. *Always alone.*

Chapter Nine

Luke didn't dream much at night when he dropped onto the old mattress they'd given him. It lay on the floor of a shed that had once served as a turkey coop — one with a five-foot-two ceiling for his six-foot height. But when he did dream, it was always a variation on the same theme — of becoming part of a pack like this one. Being an insider. Being trusted and trusting of others.

That was the stuff of his dreams.

That, and Carly. He dreamed of her, and not just at night. He'd see her coming and going around the ranch, and his heart would stop each time. Her step hitched, too, but she always hurried on with whatever odd jobs she was busy with. Even when he didn't see her, her scent would come wafting over to drive him wild. Like she sent it there, or maybe fate did.

"Not miserable at all," he'd murmur, toss and turn, and try to get some sleep.

But the pull, the drive, the craving for Carly grew more intense every day, until her scent was everywhere, teasing him, another trial for him to endure.

Want her. Need her. Now, his wolf growled.

He closed his eyes, sniffed the night, and wondered if he'd ever get to talk to her again. Wondering what he might say if he could.

Hey, honey. Check me out, turning over my new leaf.

He punched his lumpy pillow a few times and forced himself back to sleep.

Days weren't much better, because his mind was just as preoccupied with her then. Where was Carly? What was she doing? Was she thinking of him?

"Right this way," Cody said on the fifth morning. "Got a whole new job for you."

He'd finished the cesspool — thank God — and the new task was an easier one, digging an irrigation ditch. Another long workday crept by, and for every minute he spent wondering whether the enemy was moving in on North Ridge, Luke spent two minutes dreaming of Carly.

"Come on. Focus," Cody said. "Quit dreaming about Audrey."

Carly, Luke's wolf howled as he swung the pickax at the rock-hard ground.

Cody grinned. "Just kidding. But it has been quieter around here, what with Audrey so busy at the hair salon. She got a whole influx of new customers, apparently."

Luke shrugged. As long as Audrey left him alone, he didn't care where she was.

Carly, his wolf whined. *Want Carly.*

What he needed was a cold shower to get his mind off her.

"What you need is a bigger pickax—" Cody started, then stopped and whipped his head toward the far end of the ranch.

"What is it?" Luke asked when Cody's eyes narrowed and his nostrils flared.

Cody held up a hand the way a person did when they didn't want their telephone conversation interrupted. But there was no telephone, which meant Cody was listening to his mate's voice in his head. All mates could do that, and packmates, too.

Yep. Just like I hear Carly sometimes, his wolf whispered.

Luke banished the beast to the back of his mind and looked at Cody. "Everything okay?"

Cody nodded, though he didn't look so sure. "I need to run over to help Heather."

Heather, Cody's mate, was the teacher in the town's tiny school. Well, if he could call Twin Moon a town. More like a...a...

Community? The word popped into his mind.

Right. A community. And he didn't belong.

The place had everything. A one-room schoolhouse full of rambunctiously happy kids. A blacksmith whose hammer rang over the still noon air. Green grass around the houses, the clang of goat bells in the fields.

These wolves had it all. And not just the physical things. They had camaraderie — that sense of pulling together for a common cause. Fighting together, sharing the joy and tears. Something his home pack used to have, a long time ago.

Home. North Ridge. A place he was supposed to be headed back to. Alone.

Cody stood and studied him for a long minute, then nodded.

"Look. This will just take a few minutes. You go get the bigger pickax, then come straight back here to finish the job. And no messing around. You got that?" His voice dropped to a threat.

Luke blinked. Maybe someone was ready to trust him after all — at least a teeny, tiny bit.

"Sure. You mean from up in the toolshed?"

Cody waved vaguely. "I'm not sure. It's either there or up by the old aqueduct. Check both."

Luke leaned on his pickax and wiped the sweat off his brow. "Aqueduct?"

Cody made a face. "Yeah, an aqueduct without water. Some old-timer had the crazy idea to tap into a natural spring, but it never panned out. It looks more like a mine, but it doesn't go far. It's up there. Up the hill and to the right, under the lip of the ridge." He pointed and gave Luke one more look of warning.

Luke made a face. "I swear I will not maul anyone in the next ten minutes or stage an overthrow of this pack. I promise I won't steal, graffiti, or set fire to anything, either. All right?"

Cody gave him one more steely look, then nodded and left.

Luke watched him go, then set off up the rise and around a bend. He tilted his chin up, savoring the feeling of freedom — relative freedom, at least.

We could take off, you know, a dark voice whispered in the back of his mind.

Yes, he could, but he wouldn't. Not when he was finally making progress. If he stuck this out another day or two, he might just leave the ranch with a slap on the back instead of a kick in the ass.

The old aqueduct wasn't hard to find, as it turned out, because the minute he turned another corner of the rugged terrain, he saw a little girl in a flower-print dress standing right in front of it, peering in.

It really did look like a mine. Six wooden boards hung at odd angles, closing the tunnel off, but the middle board had fallen on one side, creating an opening.

"Tana!" the little girl called inside. "You know we're not allowed."

Luke slowed down. What was going on?

"Hurry up, Tana," the girl in the flower-print dress said, wringing her hands and stepping from foot to foot.

That was Cody's daughter, he knew. But what was she doing?

"Hiya," he said as quietly as he could, figuring he'd already scared enough kids on this ranch.

The little girl whirled, her eyes wide. "Hi."

Caught with a hand in the cookie jar, from the looks of it.

"What's your name?" he said, coming up beside her and peeking into the shaft.

"Holly."

"Hi, Holly. I'm Luke. Who's in there?"

"Um… no one?"

He grinned. Man, was she a bad liar. "You sure about that?"

Her chin dropped to her chest. "You promise not to tell?"

"Promise."

"Tana went in. I told her not to."

He shifted the board so he could see better, but damn, was it dark in there. "Hello?"

"Look what I found! Look!" a tiny voice echoed from inside.

He recognized Tana — Ty Hawthorne's oldest kid. And, man, it really didn't seem like a good idea for her to be in there all by herself, so he called in to her.

"Why don't you bring it out here?"

"It's stuck," she called, struggling with something.

The ceiling of the shaft groaned and creaked, making him freeze. Holy shit. The rotten beams were barely holding up the tunnel. It could collapse any minute.

"Don't touch anything!" he said. "Don't!"

"But I almost have it..."

Another creak. Jesus, the whole shaft sounded unstable. What if it came crashing down?

"Don't move. Please. Don't move."

"But I can get it," she insisted.

A dim light swung his way, then back into the darkness. A flashlight at the end of its battery life.

The roof moaned.

The sane thing to do would be to coax her out slowly or run to get someone the stubborn kid would listen to.

This is not your problem, a dark voice in his head said.

He cursed under his breath and maneuvered his body between the boards, entering the cool shade of the shaft. No way was he leaving that kid in that tunnel alone.

"Just wait a second," he said. "I'll be right there." *And then I'll carry you out of this deathtrap, if that's what it takes.*

He hunched and stepped slowly forward, running a hand lightly along one wall for orientation. Moist bits of rotting wood came up under his nails as he stepped forward.

"I think it's gold!" Tana said.

She was so excited, he couldn't really get mad. Not when he remembered all the times he'd gone exploring as a kid. He'd gotten into a few messes in his time, even a few as iffy as this.

The next overhead board sagged in the middle, and he ducked under it, afraid that any sound would bring the whole roof down. Crap, didn't Tana know how dangerous this tunnel was?

No, he realized. She had no idea. She was just a little kid.

"Look what I found! Look!"

The earth moaned above, and his blood ran cold. Jesus, did he have a bad feeling about this.

He maneuvered around a board half blocking the shaft as quickly as he dared. His eyes adjusted gradually, and there she was — a pint-sized bundle of mischief not so different than the kid he'd once been.

"See?" Tana gushed, blissfully unaware of the danger. "I think there's gold back there. But it's stuck." She jumped for a beam hanging from the ceiling.

"Don't touch!" he shouted.

Too late. Tana grabbed the protruding piece and toppled back to the ground.

Dust showered on his head as the earth around them moaned louder than before. A moan that grew into a deep rumble.

"Uh-oh," she murmured.

He reached for her hand. "Come on. Time to get out."

Thankfully, the kid didn't resist. Quick as a goat, she skipped ahead of him.

"Good girl," he murmured, eyeing the ceiling. "Just watch you don't trip—"

Her foot caught against a board that was blocking the shaft, dragging it with her, and a mighty crack sounded.

"Quick—" he started, but it was too late.

Rocks and dirt rained on him from above. He dove forward and grabbed Tana, then scrambled to the low point in the tunnel. The sunlight at the end of the shaft grew dim from all the dust raining down. One beam after another dropped, blocking their escape. If he ran for it now, he and Tana would both be crushed flat.

He shoved Tana between his feet and tented her with his body as the rest of the ceiling came crashing down.

"Cover your mouth! Stay down!"

The beams overhead were low enough to lean his back against while he braced his feet against the onslaught from above.

Tana squeaked. Holly screamed. Everything shook.

"Holly, run! Run for help!" he yelled, hoping she could hear him above the din. "Go!"

He thrust his arms out to the sides as the world went dark. Something moved beside his ankle — the only soft element in that edgy, splintered tunnel of hell. That had to be Tana, cowering by his feet. He gritted his teeth. He would not — could not — give in to the crushing force.

It was like being inside an earthquake. A rock slide. A ruthless tectonic plate. His ears roared with the sound of it. Every muscle in his back groaned and his arms shook. He ducked his chin, sheltering his mouth and nose from waves of dust. It was sheer chaos until everything went still.

Deathly still.

He blinked but couldn't tell whether he'd gotten his eyes open or not. It was that dark.

"You okay?" he whispered, praying for an answer.

Panic wasn't something he could ever remember feeling, but he sure came close when Tana didn't reply.

"Tana!" he cried.

A whimper, a scratch. God, was she all right?

"Are you hurt?" he asked, ignoring his own aching joints.

"No," a shaky voice came.

"You sure?" He found himself pleading with fate. *Please, please, let the kid be all right.* She had her whole life ahead of her — if he could hold the ceiling up long enough. If help arrived quickly to dig them out of that dank grave.

If, if, if.

"I'm not hurt," Tana said, then started crying softly.

He figured it was from fright, but then she whispered through her tears.

"Don't tell my daddy. Please don't tell my daddy."

He gnashed his teeth. Ty Hawthorne didn't seem like an abusive father, but you could never tell. "Why? Does he get mad?"

Luke found himself vowing to kill the man if he ever made it out of this hellhole alive.

"Not mad. Disappointed." Her voice wavered. "You promise not to tell?"

He let out a puff of air. So that's what it was. It couldn't be easy for the alpha's kid, shouldering so much pressure. A self-imposed pressure, it seemed — that drive to be the best. Yeah, he remembered that. Wanting to be as tough as his dad and uncle. Tougher, even. But he'd never gotten his chance.

The sniffling went on while he struggled to answer. "Sweetheart, I think your dad is going to find out."

She curled into an even tighter ball and sniffed harder.

"But he won't be mad. He'll just be glad to see you. Believe me."

"You think so?"

He thought about it for a second, because he didn't want to lie to a kid. Then he nodded. He'd seen Ty Hawthorne's eyes grow soft when he looked at his kids. And when Ty turned back to work, his gaze would harden and grow fierce in an *I will do anything to protect my family* glare.

"I know it." He nodded. "What we have to do is stay still and hang on. Help will come soon."

Okay, so he wasn't so sure about the *soon* part. How fast could Holly run? How long would this little pocket of air last?

"Just hang in there," he murmured, as much to himself as to Tana.

He shifted slightly, trying to avoid the sharp edge of a beam that was digging into his back. The needle points of a dozen splinters cut into his palms, but he didn't dare adjust the way his hands were braced against the walls of the tunnel. The A-frame of his body was the only thing keeping the rest of the tunnel from collapsing on Tana right now.

Every bone in his body screamed. His muscles shook, and his teeth hurt from clenching against the pain pulsing through his body. The earth above him shifted, trying to squeeze the resistance out of him, but he pushed back harder. He could not — would not — fail.

But crap, would it be close.

He counted seconds, then minutes, then decided he'd better not count any more.

"You know any good songs?" he asked. Maybe that would keep him going. Maybe it would help keep Tana going, too.

She hesitated, then started singing so quietly, he could barely hear. "I know a mule, her name is Sal..."

He smiled in spite of himself. His sister used to sing that one, too.

His sister. He gritted his teeth harder and pushed back against the memories.

"She's a good old worker and a good old pal..."

He hummed along with that tune, and the next one Tana came up with, and the next.

"This land is your land, this land is my land—" Tana stopped abruptly as the earth rumbled again.

Luke clenched every muscle in his body and closed his eyes, picturing the forces that would crush their tiny shelter to nothingness.

But it wasn't the earth around them shaking. There were footsteps outside.

"Tana?" a woman called, panic tight in her voice. "Tana?"

"Mommy!" she cried.

Luke was tempted to cry the same way.

He'd never have thought it possible, but when Ty Hawthorne's gritty voice boomed into the tunnel, it trembled with fear.

"Tana!"

Luke's legs trembled in the same way. If they didn't hurry up...

"We're coming. Just keep still," they called.

More voices joined those outside. Rock dragged against rock. The dust stirred again as a whiff of fresh air wandered in. Shovels scraped, and wood creaked.

"Watch it!" Luke hissed, fearful they'd bring the whole place down. "Keep it slow."

An eternity passed, but then a rock was rolled aside, casting a shaft of light on his feet. Tana scooted to freedom through the tiny space. And Luke — for a split second, his heart sank. What if they left him there?

He'd die. Plain and simple. Was he ready for that?

His arms shook, and he nearly let the mountain end it all. Now that the kid was safe, what did he really have to live for?

An image of Carly popped into his mind, but he forced it away. She deserved better than him. Way better.

Then his mind wandered to all the sins he still had to atone for, and he straightened a little bit. No, he wasn't ready to die. Not like this. He'd only just started making up for the mistakes in his past. He couldn't stop now.

So he whispered a word he hadn't used for a long, long time.

"Help." *Please help. Quickly,* he pleaded inside.

"Hang on." A voice knotted with concentration reached him. The low, dangerous baritone of Ty Hawthorne.

His muscles groaned back. *Can't hang on.*

He shut his eyes and told himself fate was throwing yet another test at him, and he'd damn well better pass. So he hung on by the skin of his teeth — teeth that bit into his lip and drew blood because it was that close.

"Careful!" Cody's voice broke into the space.

Patches of darkness appeared before Luke's eyes. Death was creeping up to him, snickering in glee.

Whatever remained of the shaft's framing groaned again. At the same time, a second beam of light pierced the darkness as another obstacle was pushed aside.

"Move it. Move!" Ty Hawthorne barked.

Luke scrambled forward as the earth thundered. One step. Two steps. A third. He clawed his way forward and tripped into blissfully open space. He rammed into Ty Hawthorne, too, but barely felt the impact. Then he was lying in the dirt, gulping fresh air and staring at the sky.

So blue. So clean. So much open space.

Dust showered out of the collapsing shaft, and someone pulled him clear. Voices shouted all around, but he didn't care. Not about the sting in his eyes or the ache in his chest. He soaked in the sight of blue sky as if it were water.

The last bit of the tunnel crumbled in on itself, and he could swear the voice of fate hissed through the din.

There, wolf, it seemed to say. *Your second chance.*

Yeah, he got the message. *Make something of it, asshole. Or else.*

It was at exactly that second that Carly raced into view. She crested the little rise that opened into that area and promptly hit the brakes.

"Whoa," she murmured, staring at him.

And just like that, he was back in a tunnel again — but a good one, with him at one end and Carly at the other, both of them bathed in golden light. His heart beat faster, and he caught a breath, savoring the clean, clear air.

The woman who laughed in the face of danger actually looked worried for a moment. She hurried toward him, touching his shoulders, checking him, whispering—

Then she pulled up short, scowled — and, *bam!* Reality hit him all over again.

She didn't want him. He'd never get the happy ending that had briefly teased his soul.

He rolled onto his stomach and coughed into the dirt for a good five minutes. Hands smacked his back, and it took him a while to figure out they weren't furious with him.

"Good job, man."

"Close call."

"Are you nuts?" Carly added, stooping beside him.

Funny to hear the local daredevil ask him that.

The ruckus settled down eventually, and he got as far as sitting up before his back screamed for him to stop. So he paused and looked around. At Carly. At the rubble blocking the aqueduct completely.

Holy shit.

"You okay?" Cody leaned over, studying him.

Luke looked past Cody to where Ty Hawthorne hugged his daughter.

"Don't be mad, Daddy," she cried.

"I'm not mad, muffin." The alpha's arms shook, and the one area of his face that wasn't smudged with dirt was pale. "I'm just scared to death."

"But nothing scares you, Daddy. Nothing."

The big alpha just hugged her tighter and held her to his chest.

"Thank you. Thank you so much," Lana Hawthorne said, patting Luke on the back.

He was sure her mate would jump between them if he saw that, but when Ty's eyes cracked open, there was no malice in them. Just gratitude. He nodded — just once, but it was enough.

Thank you, that nod said.

Luke looked away before the alpha went back to his usual distrusting scowl.

"Are you okay?" Cody repeated.

But his voice sounded far away, like everyone else. Spots danced in front of Luke's eyes, and the only thing he could really focus on was Carly. He searched her eyes for the flash of concern he'd seen before. The sparkle of interest.

And, *zing!* There it was, a spark of gold in her bright blue eyes.

"Yeah," he nodded, choking on his words. Yeah, he was okay now.

Chapter Ten

Never in a hundred adventures and misadventures had Carly's heart beat as frantically as it did then. Not even in the closest of her close calls. Her heart was skipping, pounding, heaving at the idea of Luke so close to certain death.

Mate! her wolf wailed. *Mate!*

She'd just about bowled Cody over in her rush to get to Luke's side, and it was only when she got there that she hit the brakes — just in time to avoid hugging him to her chest.

Whoa. Wait a second. What was she doing, rushing up to him like that?

He's our mate, her wolf cried. *Our mate could have died.*

She tried shaking her head. She didn't have a mate.

Then how did we know something was wrong from so far away?

That one, she didn't have an answer for. And it was hard to kid herself with her heart still jackhammering in her chest. She really had sensed Luke's distress from all the way across the ranch. She'd run as fast as she could, and instinct had brought her right to the aqueduct.

Instinct brought us to our mate, her wolf said.

"Come here, sweetie," Lana said, peeling Tana away from Ty and hugging her daughter tightly. "Let's go home."

Within minutes, everyone filed away, focused entirely on the kids. Which left Carly alone with Luke. She wanted to take off before the same overwhelming urge to touch him set in as it had that night they'd met in the bar. But, shit. She wanted to stay, too.

Can't leave him now! Not when he's hurt.

"You okay?" She couldn't help it — she put her hand on his back. A big mistake, as it turned out, because, *zing!* Even that contact made her body sing.

Careful, her wolf cried. *Mate is hurt.*

When Cody had dusted him off, Luke had winced. Now, he was just about swaying on his feet.

"Perfect," Luke muttered just as his knees buckled.

She slid her arm around his torso and propped him up. "Right. Sure."

Well, he is perfect, her wolf murmured, feeling the hard bulk of him flex.

"I'm fine," he said through clenched teeth. His eyes were closed as if the world might be spinning in his mind.

"Right," she said, adjusting her grip. "Come this way, Superman."

"I'm fine."

"Yeah, I can see that."

She guided him along far more gently than she meant to. The heat of his body crept over to hers, and no matter how hard she tried to pretend she didn't notice, she did.

It felt good. Comforting. Right.

He exhaled and relaxed under her grip. Was he thinking the same thing?

Boy, was destiny playing some mean tricks. Like inundating her with his musky scent. Like giving him that lost puppy look she sometimes spied when he let his guard down.

His guard is down because he's with us, her wolf said. *He trusts us.*

Well, she sure as hell didn't trust him — or herself.

She did some quick calculating. There was no way she could abandon Luke at that shack he'd been staying in. And no matter how she was tempted to bring him to the place she was staying in — Tina's old place — she wasn't about to succumb and do that. But the little adobe guest house was empty, and it had just what Luke needed — a shower and a nice cozy bed.

A nice big bed. Her wolf nodded eagerly.

All we're doing is helping him get there. This big, bad wolf can handle the rest on his own.

Our big, bad wolf, her inner beast sighed.

She steered him down the hill and across the ranch. The setting sun cast a rich, golden glow over the scene, but her focus was on the layer of dust and sweat caking Luke's skin.

My poor mate. My poor mate, her wolf kept fretting.

Part of her hoped Aunt Jean or someone else would appear, cluck over Luke, and insist on caring for him. But everyone had gone off to check the kids, and the ranch was quiet. So quiet, she could hear destiny whispering from across the plains.

This is no accident. This man is your mate.

She bit her lip. If only the contact didn't feel so good. So right. If only her soul didn't skip and sing from holding him close.

"Almost there," she murmured, forcing herself to take long, even breaths. The longer she spent with Luke pressed against her side, the more her wolf threatened to take over, and who knew where that might lead?

They wound past the old barn that had been converted into a community hall and past the gnarled old juniper that she'd climbed as a kid. And she found herself itching to tell Luke about each little landmark, each different place.

Every time I got to visit the ranch when I was little, I used to jump between those tree stumps. See them? And over there — you see the crawl space under the supply shed? When I was five, I followed a skunk in there to see if he was a shifter, too. Cody got me out before I got sprayed, and I made him swear never to tell.

Would Luke like to hear those stories? Would he even care? She'd never waxed poetic about the ranch to anyone before, and suddenly, she wanted to share all her feelings about the people and the place at once.

I love the ranch. I love and hate it because I belong, but I don't belong. My brothers and sister got to grow up here, while I had to follow my mom around. My roots are here, but I'm a tumbleweed.

She'd considered moving to the ranch a dozen times in the past few years, but somehow, it felt like that wasn't right. Like something bigger and better was waiting for her out there.

A zephyr of wind stirred the acacia to her right, and she swore she heard a whisper in the movement. *Something like him.*

Luke leaned heavily on her, close enough for his breath to tickle her hair. Close enough for her to imagine getting a hell of a lot closer if only she could. Face-to-face. Skin-to-skin. Heart-to-heart.

"This is the guest house," she said, waving at the historic little adobe in the middle of the ranch. She tried to play it cool while desperately scrambling to remember her plan. She did have a plan, right?

Oh, I have a plan, all right, her wolf murmured.

"You can shower here," she said, keeping up her side of the conversation.

"Nice," Luke mumbled, so low her toes curled.

Nice, her wolf agreed, keeping him snug against her side.

"So, here we are," she said, pushing the rusty door open with a screech.

Luke broke away from her as she breezed into the familiar one-room space. She'd stayed there occasionally, but somehow, the place had a whole different vibe to it this time. A secret, sensual vibe. The high ceiling promised to keep her most intimate secrets, and the crisp white linens on the bed practically purred for her to come over and rest with Luke.

She shook her head. No way. She was just dropping him off, right?

He needs us, her wolf cried.

A painting of a red rose hung over the bed. She knew every contour of every petal, but there was a new, blatantly suggestive aspect to it she'd never picked up on before.

The screen door closed with a dull thwack, and she turned around.

Luke leaned heavily against the doorframe. "Nice," he murmured again. His eyes were shut though, and his face pinched.

Her wolf whined, and Carly had to fight hard not to rush to his side and stroke his arm.

He needs us. Plus, Aunt Jean would kill you if you let him get into the bed all grimy like that.

She pursed her lips. Maybe the wolf had a point.

"You'll find everything you need for a shower..." She motioned toward the bathroom, then trailed off. She'd never seen a man more tired.

"Thanks," he mumbled quietly. "That's great."

Carly stuck her hands on her hips. It was not great, damn it. She couldn't leave him, but she sure as hell couldn't stay, much less help him into the shower.

Why not? her wolf said, licking its lips. *It's not like we've never seen him naked.*

That was different. That was back when he was a harmless stranger she thought she'd never see again. Back before the defenses around her heart had started to crack.

He saved Tana. It's only right to pay him back, her wolf argued.

She squeezed her lips together, then took a deep breath. Fine. She'd guide him into the shower, which was bound to perk him up a little—

Her wolf nodded eagerly. *Sure. Right. Perk him up.*

—and then he could take care of the rest on his own.

"Okay, okay," she mumbled, giving in at last. "Come on."

"I'm fine."

"Move it, Hot Stuff." Her words were sharp, but she made sure her grip on his arm was gentle.

Luke half stumbled, half lurched toward the bathroom and stood with both arms propped heavily on either side of the sink.

Shit. She really was going to have to help him into the shower.

"So, your shirt," she tried. When he didn't move, she pulled the hem out of his jeans and slowly worked it up his torso. Dust rained down from the movement, reminding her how close he'd come to being buried alive. Her hands tingled on first contact with his skin, and her face heated. But the second she spotted the first bruises...

"Whoa. Luke," she gasped.

Because it wasn't just one or two, but a whole patchwork of them, blue and purple and hot to the touch. Some were even darker than the tribal tattoos etched into his skin in thick lines. Together, the bruises and tattoos formed a scene more menacing than the most powerful clouds of a summer monsoon swirling angrily across the sky.

"Not so bad." He grimaced as she pulled the shirt over his shoulders.

"Not so bad, my ass." The few areas of his shoulders that weren't bruised were scratched and cut.

"Shifter healing," he murmured.

She stopped abruptly, realizing how many times she'd said the same thing. Like the time she crashed her first Harley — and the second. The time she'd plummeted fifty feet when a rock-climbing move went badly wrong. When she'd limped home from each of those incidents, her mother or sister or aunt would look at her, wide-eyed with fear.

Shifter healing, she'd said each time.

She'd always been so intent on hiding the pain that their concern was more annoying than heartwarming. And she'd never understood why they seemed so invested when everything turned out all right.

But what if it didn't? her mother had gasped, clutching her shoulders.

Carly, what if you died? Tina had once asked, looking white as a sheet.

Carly stood perfectly still, replaying the moment when Luke had stumbled out of the shaft half a second before the whole tunnel caved in, and her heart lurched again. She'd never been so scared in her life. She'd never been so scared of losing someone she loved.

Sure, her siblings and father had all been in mortal danger at one time or another, but she hadn't witnessed those occasions. She'd never really thought about what it meant to have one of them erased from her life.

But now, it was all she could think about. What if Luke had died? What if she lost him forever? What if...

She blinked and looked up when something tightened over her hand. It was Luke, looking at her in the mirror. "It's not that bad."

The same bullshit line she'd told her loved ones, once upon a time.

She tossed his shirt aside and reached around his waist for the button of his jeans. The movement came smoothly, naturally, and even with Luke's eyes steady on her, she didn't feel self-conscious.

Why should we? He's our mate.

If he's sporting a major hard-on, I'm out of here, she warned her wolf. *It will just show he's a fake.*

He wasn't a fake, as it turned out, leaving her strangely disappointed — and doubly concerned. He winced and stepped stiffly out of his boots, jeans, and boxers, holding on to the sink the whole time.

She turned on the shower tap, tested the water, and guided him in.

"See? Nice and warm." For some reason, her words came out in a soft, *you-poor-puppy* tone.

Luke stood under the flow of water, bracing his hands against the shower wall while his head hung low. A solid slab of muscle that might as well have been a statue — he was that motionless, that silent.

"The soap's right there." She pointed, but he didn't stir. Water ran along the contours of his body, emphasizing the dark curves of his tattoos.

"And shampoo..." she tried.

He didn't move an inch.

We have to help him, her wolf insisted.

She bit her lip. If she gave in now...

But not giving in was just as bad, because it wasn't just about her. It was about him. For the past few days, he'd labored away at the worst jobs on the ranch without complaint. He'd held his tongue and somehow held on to his pride.

She stared at him. From the outside, this man exuded *bad boy* vibes. But on the inside, he was all heart. All determination. All...good.

A man of honor, her wolf hummed. *We have to help him,* her wolf cried.

Unnecessarily, as it turned out, because she was already working down the buttons of her shirt. A second later, she stripped out of her jeans and stepped into the shower behind him.

Just helping him, she told herself, wondering if it was a lie. *Just helping him.*

Chapter Eleven

Carly reached for the soap and ran a hand gingerly down Luke's back.

"Is this okay?" she asked.

He nodded quietly.

She closed her eyes for a moment. Christ, she was so, so close to him. The only thing separating her hips from the steely curve of his ass was a thin cascade of water and a hairsbreadth of space.

Her nipples instantly peaked, and her core warmed. This was going to be torture.

She slid the soap over his back and gently spread the suds with her free hand.

"Feels good," he whispered hoarsely.

Sure does, she almost said.

Her hand glided over the S curve of his back, from the broad expanse of his shoulders down the line of his spine and over his rear. Then she raised her hand and started all over again, erasing all the grime, memorizing every curve. Her nostrils flared the way they did when she was about to rev her motorcycle or attempt a new rock face.

Danger, her body cried all too eagerly. *Danger.*

No danger, her wolf whispered.

Of course, there was. She could lose everything to this man. Her heart. Her independence. Her soul.

He can give you more, the deep voice of fate whispered in her mind. *Love. Light. Direction.*

Luke stiffened when she touched a sore spot, then relaxed under her touch again. He even sighed, as she nearly did.

Whoever had done his tattoos was a master of the art. The dark lines curved in harmony with the lines of his body — bold swirls over his shoulder blades, jagged lightning bolts along his ribs. Interlocking knots unfurled into long, streaming whips. Some lines were pure black, while others were made of countless tiny hash marks offset by ninety degrees.

Offset by bruises, too, but as the shower steamed up, the worst of them began to fade.

Shifter healing. Her wolf grinned.

Her strokes dropped lower, dipping down to his hips and along his ass. She tilted her shoulders to reach as low as his thighs, and when she straightened, their bodies brushed. The tingles of electricity zapping around her body all exploded at the same time, and she sucked in a deep breath.

Luke did, too.

She did it again, starting by tilting her right shoulder down and resting her left hand lightly on his hip. Her fingers massaged slowly on the downstroke, featherlight on the upstroke, moving closer to the front of his body this time. And when she straightened, her nipples skipped in and out of contact with his skin.

Her wolf just about threw back its head and howled, it felt that good.

Of course, she was supposed to be taking care of Luke, not living out a fantasy, but it was too hard to resist. Damn near impossible, in fact, so she did it again. This time with a hand on each of his hips, traveling slowly down...

Down...

Down.

Her hands curved forward slightly as she imagined touching his cock. Playing with it gently, rubbing up and down.

When she came up again, brushing her chest along his back the whole way, Luke's head wasn't hanging low. It was up. Still facing the wall, but definitely more alert.

"You want me to stop?" she whispered.

He shuffled a little, spreading his legs in a tiny but unmistakable gesture.

"I never want you to stop," he murmured in a voice so low, she nearly missed it.

She pressed her cheek to his shoulder and closed her eyes. Was she really going to allow herself to do this?

Her wolf wasn't the only voice answering with a *Hell, yes!* Her soul screamed it, too.

She lathered up her hands and dipped down again. The line of his ribs guided her hands to his rear, where she followed the flow of water along his ass. She bent low enough to kiss his lower back, and when she straightened, she didn't stand so much as climb his body, rubbing every inch of his skin. Her hands slid forward, brushing against the hard jut of his cock.

Carly grinned in spite of herself. The shower was definitely perking him up.

Luke pushed backward slightly, seeking more contact. And the next time she repeated the long, sensual slide, he put his hands over hers and guided them right to his cock.

He didn't say a word, but when she took his steel-hard shaft in her hand, he tipped his head back and held his breath.

She paused long enough to lather up well — cheap excuse — and stroked up, down, and around his cock until every last sud had been carried away by the water streaming from overhead.

The fire inside her crackled and swirled, and her thoughts melted into each other until the only message that got through was a primal, needy one.

Want this man, her wolf growled. *Need this man.*

He needs us, too, her human side agreed, on board at last.

Luke caught her hands and turned slowly around. His deep, dark eyes shone in the dim light, and the muscles of his face were hard. His lips opened a crack.

So close, her body screamed. Close enough to kiss.

"Last chance," he whispered.

"Last chance for what?" she asked, trying to play it cool. Bracing herself for an epic fail, because she was close to dropping to her knees to beg — or better yet, to lick and taste.

"Last chance for you to leave before we do something you regret."

His hands gripped hers firmly yet gently. The pain had gone from his eyes, replaced by a need she was sure her eyes showed, too.

She leaned in closer, bringing her lips within an inch of his. "Would you regret this?"

He was so close, he had to tip his chin down to maintain eye contact. "Never."

His voice was hoarse but firm. So firm, it ought to have set off every alarm in her body. When a powerful he-wolf decided something was his, he'd never give up the pursuit of it. Never. Was she ready for that?

She held herself in check just long enough to ascertain that she didn't give a damn. Not with her core weeping, her nipples hardening, her mouth starving for him.

"No regrets," she murmured, tipping her chin up.

I'll hold you to that, her wolf murmured as she gently wrapped her arms around his neck and covered his mouth with hers.

Remember, her wolf said. *No regrets.*

She was ready to promise anything to anybody at that point. Her Triumph. Her first-born child. Her soul to the devil. She'd been fighting destiny all week, and she was finally ready to admit defeat.

No regrets, she told herself, losing herself in the kiss.

It was more of a full-frontal attack than a kiss, but Luke didn't seem to mind. His lips parted, yielding to her tongue, and he pulled her body snugly against his chest. So snug, she could have wrapped her legs around him and gone airborne, leaving the standing to him.

She settled for grinding against his erection and whimpering out loud.

So good. So good. . .

Whether that was her wolf moaning in pleasure or her human side, she couldn't tell. All she cared about was getting closer. She angled her head right and Luke did the same, and their tongues tangled. Their hands tangled, too — hers, seeking the thick heat of his cock, while his plowed down her rear in long, hard strokes.

Strokes that said, *Mine. Mine. Mine.*

Strokes that echoed the sweep of her lips and craving tongue. *Mine.*

When she reached blindly for the tap and turned the water off, she was already thinking ahead to toweling Luke off and dragging him to the bed. But when she eased away, he turned and pinned her body between his and the tiled wall.

"Not yet," he whispered. "Not yet."

Water streamed off his shoulders and onto hers. Heat flared back and forth between their bodies in uncontrollable bursts as he took over the kiss. His tongue reached deeper, and his lips plucked even more desperately than hers had at his.

"Need this," he whispered. "Need you."

When he lifted her arms and held them high over her head, capturing her completely, the last droplets of water ran in slow, lazy lines along her breasts.

Let me guess, she said, trying to keep a little sass in her voice. *Shifter healing has finally kicked in.*

He nodded through the kiss, pulling her head up and down with his. *Let me prove it to you.*

Before she could respond, he ducked and sealed his mouth over her neck, nipping, sucking, and licking until she was writhing in his arms. His hands kept hers captive, and it didn't bother her that she couldn't tug free. She was enjoying the play-struggle far too much.

Maybe she wanted to be captured. Maybe she wanted to be possessed.

She pressed her hips closer to Luke's. When he stiffened and hissed into her ear, her grin grew. Maybe he liked being captured, too. Because the lean and tilt of his hips wasn't so much a struggle as an erotic dance for two.

She stretched her torso, pulling her breasts along his chest, then sank down again, seeking the best connection of all.

"Luke," she whispered.

"Not yet," he murmured, dipping lower. His tongue flicked along her breast, taunting her nipple until he caught it and nipped.

She howled and arched within his grip, desperate to be filled. "Luke," she moaned.

He twisted and sucked her nipple harder, and she shook in his arms. She was close to climaxing already, damn it, and he hadn't even touched her where she needed him most yet.

"Not yet," he murmured, though his voice shook this time.

He switched to the other breast and worked it hard while his warm, wide hand pressed between her legs.

"Right there," she murmured, rocking against him.

Her hips were still tight against his, so he didn't have much space — on the outside, that is. Inside, she was wide and slick and practically weeping for him. He teased her for a minute longer until his breath came in short pants, much like hers.

"Luke. Please," she begged.

He held her nipple in his mouth a moment longer, stroking the underside with his tongue, then slowly straightened until they were face-to-face. He kissed her so long and hard, she couldn't see straight. Everything became vague and blurry, and she was barely aware of Luke tipping right.

"Towel," he murmured.

"Towel?"

"Need to get you to that bed."

She forced herself back to her senses as he whisked the towel over her back.

"You sure you're okay?" she managed. "If this is too much..."

He broke her off with a searing kiss. "Don't even think about stopping now." He wrapped the towel around her and kissed her all the way over to the bedroom. "Don't...even...think...about...it."

When her legs bumped the bed frame, she pulled the towel out of his hands and wiped him dry — thoroughly.

Shifter healing, her wolf murmured as she dabbed at his chest. The bruises were still there, but not quite as colorful as before.

She scrubbed his hair, grinning at the way it spiked up.

"I think I'm dry enough," he murmured, cupping her breasts.

She grinned and gently elbowed herself free. "Gotta make sure, you know." She ran the towel down his belly, then up and down his shaft.

He closed his eyes, letting her play with him. His head rolled back, and his fists clenched at his sides. Obviously, she wasn't the only one enjoying such a simple act. When his eyes snapped open, they glowed.

He pulled the towel out of her hands and patted the bed. "Lie back."

"Make me," she retorted, half challenge, half tease.

He smiled that devastating smile. "I'll make you want to."

The husky note in his voice alone made her want to drop flat on her back. And when he started kissing her, she was a goner all over again.

"Lie back," he whispered, all hoarse and gritty.

She leaned back, hanging on to him. Spreading her legs as she went. Luke followed, coming down on top of her, kissing her breast while reaching between her legs.

"Yes..." she whispered, arching her back.

His fingers swept back and forth across her folds, opening her.

"Yes," she cried as he fingered her inside.

One finger. Two fingers. Three, and she still wasn't satisfied.

"Luke," she panted.

His breath came in impatient little puffs, too, but still, he teased her.

"I need you inside me," she begged. "Need you so bad..."

She wrapped her legs around him as he crawled up her body. She moaned and wiggled, willing his cock into position at her core.

His nostrils widened as he hitched her leg higher, keeping it nice and tight against his side. She braced herself for him to penetrate, but he paused and looked at her.

"No regrets?" Luke asked, looking as serious as she'd ever seen him.

His gritty voice was full of need — and barely hidden beneath that, pain and uncertainty. Enough to make her soul cry out for him.

She locked eyes on his and shook her head quickly. "No regrets."

"No leaving without saying good-bye."

That caught her by surprise. Had she hurt him by sneaking out that morning after their meeting at the bar?

She shook her head in solemn promise. "No leaving without saying good-bye."

A good thing he didn't ask her never to leave, period, because she just might have promised that, too.

He nodded, and his eyes narrowed on her face. A quiet second slipped by, just long enough to have squeezed in three little words if either of them had had the nerve to.

I love you.

She saw the words on the tip of his tongue as surely as she felt them on her own. Then his lips parted, and his teeth came together in a tiny signal of warning. His cock twitched against the soft flesh of her core.

"Please," she urged.

When Luke planted his hands beside either side of her head, Carly braced herself, knowing when he came, it would be hard, hot, and deep.

Chapter Twelve

"Please," Carly whispered.

A ripple of need pulsed through Luke's body, and he knew he couldn't hold back long. Just long enough to memorize this moment so he could cherish it for a lifetime.

It was insane, the effect Carly had on him. Just hearing her utter his name blinded him with desire. It made him forget that caught-at-the-doorway-to-hell feeling he'd had when he was trapped inside the collapsing aqueduct. It made him forget the weary labor of the past week, too. He truly had reached the point of lonely misery.

But then Carly had come along with her soft hands, silky hair, and gentle voice — the first time she'd spoken to him that way. The first time anyone had spoken to him that way in a long, long time, in fact. Maybe the first time he'd listened hard enough to catch the wobble of concern, the scratch of terror in her tone.

And now, to catch the raw need in her words.

"Need you," she pleaded, squirming against him. "Please."

Her words were his command. He hammered into her, eliciting a wild howl from his inner wolf.

God, she was so tight. So perfect. So beautiful. And she was all his.

Carly hissed and tipped her head back, her lips moving with a cry of pleasure that echoed in his head. Her hair fanned out around the pillow, still wet in places, gold and silky in others. Her nipples peaked against his chest, pink and rosy and hard. Her legs held his hips tightly, ready for a wild ride. All week, he'd been dreaming of her.

Not dreaming any more, his wolf howled.

He pulled back and plunged forward again, relishing the squeeze around his cock, the give as she stretched around him.

"Luke," she groaned, digging her nails into his shoulders.

More, her wolf cried into his mind. *More.*

In his dreams, he'd taken his time to tease and torture her. In his dreams, he'd made her come multiple times before plunging in.

In reality, he pumped wildly, crazy with need. His mind emptied of all the different fantasies he'd harbored — the positions he wanted to tease her with, the whispered confessions he needed to get off his chest, the slow, lazy lovemaking he'd pictured sharing with her. But this was instinctive. Animal. Almost edging toward survival, as if his entire future — and hers — hinged on the two of them coming to a screaming high at exactly the same time.

It does, a deep, dark voice whispered in his mind. *Take her. Make her yours right now.*

"Yes," she moaned, bucking against him. Was she agreeing with the voice of destiny, or was it just a word?

Every time she squeezed her inner muscles around his cock, it burned. A burn he couldn't get enough of, so he withdrew and plunged back in to feel it all over again.

"Yes... Yes..." she panted.

His heart hammered. The last bead of water — or the first drop of sweat — fell from his chest to hers and glistened there.

Take her, the earthy voice commanded. *Make her yours.*

His canines ached, begging to extend. Carly tipped her head back, exposing her neck.

This is your mate. One bite will bind her to you forever. Don't wait, that scratchy voice said.

A roar built up in his ears, and his body screamed for release.

Take her. Make her ours, his wolf howled.

He eyed her neck as his hips pumped on, getting a feel for the timing so he could plunge his teeth into her and deliver the mating bite.

So, so easy. She's ours, his wolf howled in glee.

His cock burned. His soul danced. But deep at the back of his mind, one tiny alarm pinged.

Mine, mine, mine. So easy—

Easy? The distraction threw him off-balance just long enough for his brain to flick on again.

Easy wasn't good. Easy wasn't lasting. Easy wasn't why he'd been working his ass off at this ranch instead of hightailing it north.

"Close," she murmured, bringing her legs higher. "I'm so close..."

His canines screamed as he forced them to recede. Better the long road to reward than a shortcut to hell, right?

His wolf cried, but his heart tapped its approval inside his chest.

"Yes," Carly cried as he found his rhythm again.

Yes. He nodded to himself. She was his destined mate.

"Yes..." Her voice shot higher.

Yes. He wanted her more than anything.

"God, yes..." she mumbled, clutching his shoulders.

He pounded harder and harder, clenching his teeth. Counting down five more slides into heaven before he'd allow himself to come.

Carly cried out as her body convulsed around his.

He gritted his teeth through the last two thrusts, then exploded into a release. White light blinded his eyes, and a deep, searing heat rushed through his body.

"Oh," Carly moaned, clamping around him in a second wave of ecstasy.

Oh, yes, he said, though all that came out was a growl.

Every muscle in his body contracted in deliriously pleasurable pain, and he folded over her body, spent.

A warm wave of satisfaction seeped through him. Carly sighed and went limp. Her hands fluttered over his back, and she mumbled incoherently as he panted against her skin.

Mate, his soul wolf hummed. *My destined mate.*

He started to roll sideways, but Carly protested. "Stay. Please stay."

He paused, relishing the soft press of her breasts against his chest, the slick heat between her legs where his cock still lay.

Why didn't you make her ours? his wolf demanded. *Why take the risk?*

Because Carly would never forgive him if he did. Because she wasn't his to take. Because she was worth it.

His wolf grumbled — but when Carly stroked his back, the beast gave itself over to pleasure again. She wrapped him in a hug that promised this wouldn't be their last night together, and the beast let out a deep sigh.

Just when he was about to drift off to sleep, Carly shifted position and kissed him. On the shoulder first, then on the neck and cheek. She propped herself up and looked down at him with shiny eyes.

"Not bad, Hot Stuff. Not bad."

"Not bad?"

She smiled, then lowered herself into a gentler version of their first, desperate kiss. This one was just as wide and deep, but slower and satisfied. Damn satisfied, just like him.

Eventually, she pulled away and got around to wiping both of them off with a corner of the sheet. Then she flopped onto the mattress and snuggled up. She stroked his back in a way that made his weary body bliss out for a while. Back and forth, back and forth. Her fingers moved over his skin. If he'd been in wolf form, he'd have rolled onto his back and thumped one leg wildly.

"I like this one," she murmured.

He cracked an eye open and found her tracing the tattoo that circled his shoulder.

"And this one," she said, moving on to the jagged lines above.

One by one, she catalogued them all. The zigzag patterns, the angry tornado whorls. The interlocking triangles around the bigger, bolder blocks. Some he had no recollection of acquiring. Others he remembered all too well.

He watched Carly, trying to keep the past in the past. But then she got to the one tattoo that wasn't entirely abstract, and he held his breath.

He'd been with women who'd studied his tattoos, but none of them got that particular one right. The big, bold circle swirled around a wolf etched in thick, separate strokes.

Oh, they'd say. *It's a wolf, howling at the moon. That's cute.*

Which always made him wince, because they couldn't be more wrong.

Carly ran her finger over that section again and again, and the smile playing around her lips faded.

"A wolf crying under the moon," she whispered sadly.

Luke went perfectly still. It figured Carly would be the one person to see that tattoo for what it was, just the way she saw him for what he was.

Her eyes flicked to his face, and he saw a question in them. *Why is he crying?*

Before he could answer, though, she put a finger on his lips and shook her head. As if she didn't need the answer, because she already knew.

The wolf was him. A wolf who hadn't quite come to terms with his ghosts or atoned for his sins.

She stroked the wolf's back as if petting it and kissed Luke softly on the brow — exactly the kind of kiss he needed just then.

"No regrets," she whispered.

He forced a thin smile. He had a shit-ton of regrets. But this night wasn't one of them, so he leaned forward and nuzzled her. Lightly at first, then harder, scrubbing her with the stubble of his jaw. Marking her as thoroughly as she marked him.

Carly's hands ran over his back then nudged toward his ass in long, lingering sweeps that hinted she was ready for more. Was he?

He rolled onto his back and motioned her closer, then captured her lips in a kiss. Hell, yes, he was ready.

He was just about to roll on top of her when she beat him to it. One surprisingly firm hand pressed him back into the mattress, and her blue eyes sparkled.

"Lie back," she ordered him.

He grinned so hard, his cheeks hurt.

"Make me," he whispered.

Her eyes dropped to his cock, and she licked her lips. "I'll make you want to."

He chuckled, settled back, and let her move over him, scattering wet kisses around the tight nub of his nipple as she went. Slowly, she moved downward, and every nerve in his body hummed in anticipation.

She'd been straddling his thigh, and as she slid down, he could feel her go wet for him in the same way his cock glistened for her.

She smacked her lips — once, twice — then stopped.

"You should see yourself, Hot Stuff," she laughed.

Spread out and powerless to resist? Cock straining for the first touch of those incredible lips? Well, he could live with that, given the woman he was handing the reins to.

"I like what I see," he murmured, noting the hunger in her eyes.

"I like what I see, too," she said, tiptoeing her fingers down his abdomen to his cock. She wrapped her hand around it and started tugging gently up and down.

He was a goner right there. And when she dipped low enough to drop out of his line of sight, he held his breath. A second later, her lips closed around his cock, and his eyes just about rolled back in their sockets.

"Good?" she asked out of the side of her mouth.

"Great," he whispered, threading his fingers through her hair to guide her back into place.

Chapter Thirteen

Luke never wanted to wake up. He could snooze his life away as long as it felt this good.

Mate, his wolf murmured, still groggy. *Mate loves me.*

Her leg wound over his, and he smiled without opening his eyes. It was morning — the kind of morning he'd pictured having after their night at the bar, back when they'd met initially.

Except for something he couldn't quite put his finger on. Some new stress had wormed its way into his gut while he lay there snoozing, and the last part of the morning wasn't entirely peaceful anymore. Something itched at the edge of his conscious, but he was so tired — and the residual bliss so good — that he slumbered right through whatever that was trying to warn him of something.

Just relax, he'd told himself, drifting back off to sleep. *For once, let yourself relax.*

And he had. Sometime later, he woke again and sniffed, ready to inhale Carly's sweet scent. But instead of sighing with pleasure, his nose crinkled. Some bad scent was registering instead. He sniffed again, stiffening despite the soft rub of a hand on his ribs.

"Morning, baby," she whispered.

He frowned. Had Carly's voice grown huskier overnight? And damn, he didn't remember her nails being that long or painted or—

When she kissed his ear — more like, licked his ear — he shuddered. Last night, Carly's touch had been an elixir. Now, it made his skin crawl.

He turned slowly to come face-to-face with her, wondering what had changed.

"Whoa," he yelped.

"Surprise, baby," a sultry voice said.

He blinked and, holy shit. That wasn't Carly's golden wave of hair. That hair had had all the life bleached out of it.

"Audrey?" He jumped clear out of the bed and slammed into a chair as the scent of her dime-store perfume hit him. "What are you doing here?"

She chuckled and batted those oversized eyelashes at him. "Surprise, baby. Did you miss me?"

Hell, no. He didn't miss her. Why would he?

Audrey's eyes dropped to his groin, and she licked her lips.

Fuck. He grabbed the towel he'd discarded the night before and wrapped it around his waist.

"I heard what happened. I came to take care of you," Audrey purred, sounding a hell of a lot like a cat purring to a mouse.

"Where's Carly?" he demanded.

For a second, his gut lurched. Had Carly left without saying good-bye? She'd promised not to.

No, wait. He remembered a sleepy kiss and a whispered, *I have to go.* Something about a field trip with the kids. Or had he been dreaming that?

Crap, had he dreamed the whole thing?

Audrey scooched across the mattress and propped her face in her hands, looking up at him far too innocently. Her shoulders were bare, her skin flushed.

"Who cares about anyone but you and me? It's just us here."

Us? He and Audrey weren't an *us* and never would be. But, shit. Had he been so out of it that he'd slept with Audrey?

No way, his wolf snarled.

He looked around the room, sniffing deeply. Carly's scent was all over the place. On the sheets, on the towel. On his skin. So, whew. All Audrey had done — so far — was curl up beside him while he was asleep — a sitting duck, in other words. He'd long since figured Audrey was a man-eater, but fuck. The woman was as low as they came, sneaking in on him like that.

Sunlight cut through the windows, and a rooster crowed. Daylight already. A mixture of exhaustion and deep, sexual satisfaction had lulled him into the soundest sleep he'd had in years. But now... He'd never felt dirtier or more used. His claws pushed under his nails, itching to punish the tramp.

"What time is it?" he asked.

Audrey brought her elbows together, plumping up the ample breasts overflowing from a lacy red bra. "No hurry, baby. We have time."

He dropped the towel, grabbed his boxers, and pulled them on. Fast.

Audrey whistled. "Now that's a sight for sore eyes. No need to hide, honey. Not from me."

He yanked his pants on wordlessly — his grimy pants from the day before, which seemed like a lifetime ago — and muttered under his breath. He'd never been closer to unleashing his claws on a woman.

"Get out," he barked through clenched teeth.

"But, baby, don't you think I deserve a reward for waiting for—"

"Out!" he shouted, though he beat her to the door, grabbing his shirt as he went. Shit, this was supposed to be an entirely different kind of morning. A nice one. Quiet, too — the first truly quiet morning he'd had in a long, long time.

He hurried away from the guest house, untangling his shirt as he went, then pulling it over his head. Clean skin, filthy shirt. Like his past and present, butting up against each other yet again.

"Luke!" The screen door slammed behind him, and Audrey scurried out along with a waft of her overwhelming perfume. She was wearing her bra, and her shirt was in her hands.

His shirt blindfolded him for a moment — thank God, because he'd already seen enough of Audrey for a lifetime — but he hurried on. The second he yanked the shirt down from his face, he pulled up short.

Oh, shit.

Cody Hawthorne stood ten steps away, scowling. Sunny Cody Hawthorne, who'd never looked more like his grouchy brother, Ty.

Cody glared at him, then flicked his eyes away just long enough to glance behind Luke.

"Audrey," Cody grunted in a flat, dangerous tone. "Go."

"I was just—" she protested.

"Go."

Luke waited for her to blurt the truth in her own defense. For her to say something like, *I didn't sleep with him. Why would I?*

But she didn't say a word. She just strutted away, her shirt limp in her hands.

Cody stood dangerously still, giving Luke the evil eye. Then he shook his head. No words. Just a bitter shake of the head that cut Luke to the bone.

I didn't... I wouldn't...

Luke wanted to shout, to explain. He'd worked his ass off for days. He'd resisted so many wrongs and even managed to get a couple of things right. He hadn't laid a hand on Audrey, and he didn't want to. Couldn't Cody see that?

Footsteps scuffed the earth to his right, but he didn't bother looking. How could this possibly get worse?

"You bastard," Carly said.

He whipped his head around. "Wait, Carly—"

Her hair was gold and shiny in the early morning light. Her skin, too. Her tan seemed even more golden beside the brown leather of his jacket — yes, she was wearing it in public, even. But her face was thunderous. She'd been carrying a steaming mug in each hand, but her elbows drooped, and coffee poured to the ground.

"What were you doing with Audrey?"

The scent of fresh coffee hit his nose, another reminder of the morning he didn't get to have.

"I just woke up. I don't know how she got in there."

He stepped toward Carly, but Cody blocked the way like a goddamn linebacker. "You don't know how she got in?" His voice was full of scorn.

"I was asleep! I didn't notice."

Carly's eyebrows flipped up in fury. "You didn't notice the difference between me and Audrey?"

He looked around. Jesus, how could he ever explain?

The anger in Carly's eyes turned up a notch. "I went to set up what I needed for the field trip as quickly as I could. I even got us breakfast. And I come back to find *this*?"

What could he say? What could he do?

She turned on her heel and stomped away.

"Carly," he tried, but Cody stepped closer, crowding him.

"I told you not to mess with my sister or anyone else in this pack." Cody tilted his head to the right. "Now, go."

At first, Luke thought Cody was throwing him off the ranch, but it was worse than that. Cody was pointing him to the council house where Ty stood, frowning murderously.

Luke glanced over his shoulder at Carly, but all he saw was the red of Cody's face.

Carly! He tried calling to her mind, and for a second, he thought he heard her hurried stride pause. *Carly, how you can believe I would have anything to do with Audrey. Why would I?*

Because all men are the same, her voice shot into his mind, full of disdain.

That's not me, he pleaded. *That's not me.*

She snorted and threw up a barrier to block any other thoughts from getting through. When she passed his truck, she all but ripped off his jacket and threw it in the back.

Carly!

The wind blew from over the hills, and a parched tumbleweed rolled past. Cody shoved him toward the council house.

"I told you not to touch my sister," Cody growled again.

Luke didn't bother looking back at him. He looked straight ahead, bracing himself to face Ty. He climbed the stairs and stepped over the threshold, squinting as he went from the bright light of day to darkness.

"You," Ty Hawthorne spat.

Luke's eyes hadn't adjusted enough for to him see more than a broad outline, but Ty's words were loud and clear.

"Here I was thinking I might thank you today," Ty started in a voice that was dangerously low.

Cody snorted behind him.

"You saved the kids. We appreciate that."

I cleared your damn cesspool and dug you a ditch, too, Luke wanted to add.

"So I'm not inclined to kill you. But I'm close."

Luke put up his hands. "I get the kid sister thing. Believe me, I do. But—"

"What do you understand?" Cody shouted back, as if he was the only man in the world with a sister.

Luke took a menacing step forward, barely holding back a punch. "I had a sister, man. Had." Did he have to go into the details?

Two skeptical looks greeted him, and something broke inside. The dam holding back the worst of his memories.

"Greer came after her."

Cody looked like he had been about to say something, but he froze at Luke's words.

"Fucking Greer. No one could stop him. Not my father. Not my uncle. Not my older brothers. Greer killed them all, and then he came for my sister."

The only sound was the creak of the floorboards as Cody shifted uncomfortably. That and the buzz of a fly against a window.

"I was a kid. I couldn't stop him. I couldn't do anything. And you know what my sister said?"

Cody and Ty didn't look like they were about to ask, so he plunged ahead. "She said, 'Don't worry. He can't get me.' She went in the back room while my mom tried holding Greer at the door, and a minute later—"

The sound of a shotgun thundered through his mind. The one his sister turned on herself.

He swallowed. Hard. The Twin Moon wolves might know the feeling of protecting someone, but did they know what it was like to stand by helplessly?

"She couldn't kill Greer with that gun, but she could kill herself."

Gun wounds weren't usually enough to kill shifters, but a barrel placed against a head would.

The room went painfully silent. Ty looked at Cody, who looked at the floor. Luke paused, raging inside. Did they get it now? Did they finally get it? He had to honor the memory of his sister by getting his ass to North Ridge and preventing anything like that from happening again.

He took a deep breath, trying to get himself back on track. Fighting with words instead of with fists sucked, though. He itched to turn into wolf form.

"Carly is an adult. She can make her own choices," he said when he'd collected his nerves.

"She makes bad choices," Ty growled, though his voice wasn't quite as menacing as before.

"Bad choices, or choices you disagree with?" Luke narrowed his eyes on Ty. "Who made you her boss?"

"I run this pack."

"And that entitles you to decide who does what?" Luke shook his head. "Then you're no better than Greer."

Ty showed his teeth, but Luke held his ground. God, did he wish it were Greer there so he could throw himself into a fight. The one battle he'd never had a chance to wage.

Cody motioned to the door. "Get out. No stops, no good-byes." He took a key off a nail behind the one desk in a corner of the room and tossed it — make that, hurled it — at Luke. "Just get in that truck of yours and go."

Luke would have protested, but he remembered the look of betrayal on Carly's face. She sure wasn't going to forgive him. Which meant there was nothing left for him here.

Luke gripped the key so hard it bit into his palm. "You going to order me not to go to North Ridge next?"

No way was he going anywhere but Colorado. These assholes weren't stopping him.

"You can go wherever the hell you like. Just don't expect a welcoming committee," Ty barked.

The two brothers exchanged looks, and fuck — Luke knew what that meant. Their father was acting alpha at North

Ridge. They'd call ahead so that when Luke arrived, he'd be turned around immediately.

Fuck. His whole plan had been to prove himself to them. He could have driven straight to North Ridge a week ago without stopping here. But no, he wanted to do the right thing. And see where that got him.

Told you, a low, edgy voice growled in the back of his mind. The one trying to pull him back to the dark side.

It was nearly enough to make him roar and rage. To lash out at Ty and Cody and anyone else who tried to stop him. But then his own words hit him and he paused.

No regrets, he'd promised Carly.

He took a deep breath. She might not keep her side of that bargain, but he would. No regrets.

He fingered the keys to his truck and stepped out the door without another word. His jeans felt grimier than ever, and his shirt stuck to his back. He was leaving Twin Moon Ranch with less than he'd started with, but hell. He'd figure something out.

Somehow.

He got in his truck, fired it up, and drove out the gate, trying not to look back. But he couldn't help it; his eyes darted to the rearview mirror, and there it was. The most peaceful corner of the planet. The place where he'd screwed everything up. Well, Audrey had done that, or at least proven how fragile trust could be.

He forced himself to look to the horizon. This was just the kick in the ass he needed to get moving. He'd dallied far too long, right?

Mate, his wolf sniffed, clawing him inside.

Yeah, his mate. The one who didn't trust him enough to see through a lie. The one who was better off without him, because what could he really offer but a broken past?

The truck bounced over a rut, kicking up a plume of dust. He was driving too fast for that dirt road, but it felt good to break one little rule. He forced his chin to stay high, but every inch of ground he covered during the drive to the highway took something out of him. What if he never succeeded? What if he never found a pack to contribute to?

The smooth asphalt of the highway did nothing for his mood. Neither did the knowledge that he was finally on his way to North Ridge. There wasn't much to look forward to any more. Nothing left of his vague hopes and dreams.

He dug his fingernails into the worn vinyl of the steering wheel, then forced himself to grab the one piece of food he had — an old apple, not entirely fit to eat — and munched it down, ordering himself not to imagine how nice a breakfast with Carly might have been. When he got down to the core, he tossed the apple out the window onto the scrubby median between the north and southbound lanes of the highway — and promptly did a double take. Was that an open gate that he had just sped past?

He craned his neck to see. That was Twin Moon Ranch property, and those wolves were fastidious about protecting their land.

The gate was already behind him, so he drove on. He had no obligation to that pack. Let their cattle wander away. Let some poachers sneak in. What did he care?

A mile later, he slowed and pulled over to the shoulder, looking straight ahead.

North. North was where he had to go. But south pulled at him like a magnet, telling him he had to check that gate.

He scowled at the dashboard. That magnet was probably Carly.

An eighteen-wheeler roared by, shaking his pickup with its draft. *Just hit the road,* it said. *Doing the right thing has gotten you nowhere.*

He spat out the open window and tapped his fingers on the gearshift. Then he glanced at the mirror.

"Screw it," he murmured, hitting the indicator for a turn. The second the highway was clear, he pulled across both northbound lanes to the south side and accelerated back the way he'd come.

Even if the Twin Moon wolves never found out he'd done them a good deed, it didn't matter. He would know. And it would only take a second, right?

For some inexplicable reason, his pulse rose as he approached the gate. Why, he didn't know. It was just one gate. No big deal, right?

He pulled over and stared at it for a full minute.

His wolf snorted inside. *Forget it. Just close the gate and get going again.*

He slid out of the cab and looked down the dirt track leading into the scrub. The gate creaked slightly in the breeze. All he had to do was push it closed and...

A scent caught in his nostrils. The scent of wolf shifter. He sniffed. One second, it was there, and the next, it was gone.

Probably nothing, his wolf decided. *Probably a whiff of one of the guards.*

He studied the ground, then knelt. One softer patch of ground held several zigzag tracks. Motorcycle tracks.

He glanced up. Some ranchers used motorcycles to get around, but other than Carly's, he'd only seen one bike on the ranch — Zack's vintage Harley. And these tracks didn't match either Carly's or Zack's tires. The ranch hands all used beat-up pickups or four-wheel ATVs. So what was with the multiple motorcycle tracks overlaid by the treads of a lightweight pickup?

Not your problem, the dark voice said.

Could mean trouble, his wolf said.

He got back in his vehicle and looked at the sky for a full minute. Then he eased the pickup into gear — forward, not reverse — and headed down the dirt lane.

Chapter Fourteen

Carly power-walked all the way to the stables, looking straight ahead. Gravel crunched under her feet, and she barely acknowledged the voices that greeted her until Aunt Jean came along.

"Good morning, sweetheart. You getting ready for the field trip?"

The field trip. She'd really been looking forward to it but, shit. Here she was, about to miss part of it. Because of Luke. Because of her own stupidity.

"I'll catch up later," she said, and damn it, her voice was as scratchy and raw as her emotions.

The field trip was the only reason she'd torn herself from Luke's side so early that morning. She was responsible for the treasure hunt, and she hadn't had time to get anything ready, what with the excitement of the aqueduct accident and what happened afterward.

She snorted to herself. Excitement. Right.

She'd even been kidding herself that Luke was worth rethinking her no-mate policy — to the point that she'd hustled right back to him as quickly as she could with a steaming mug of coffee she was sure he'd appreciate. But what had the bastard been doing while she was gone?

She picked up her pace, heading uphill.

"Sweetheart, wait."

Anybody else, Carly would have brushed off. But Aunt Jean was special. Different. A surrogate mother to half the wolves on the ranch, and the former schoolteacher in the one-room schoolhouse Carly always wished she'd been able to attend like all her siblings had.

"Are you all right?"

"Sure." Carly scowled. "Great."

Maybe she ought to feel great, because up until the point she'd seen Audrey with Luke, she'd been harboring all kinds of delusions, like how nice it would be to have a mate. Someone to lean on when she needed it. Someone to wake up with. Someone to share good and bad with.

"I saw what happened," Aunt Jean said gently.

Carly stopped and looked at her feet. What did Aunt Jean mean? Had she seen Luke welcome Audrey in? Luke pretending to be innocent? Had she seen the coffee drain slowly into the dirt when Carly realized what was going on?

Carly started walking again. "Look, can you tell Heather I'll catch up with the group at the creek crossing? I'll be there in time for the treasure hunt. Right now, I need to clear my head."

And her heart, too. There were way too many false hopes and dreams in there.

"Carly, wait." Aunt Jean's voice was soft but commanding at the same time.

Carly stopped but didn't turn around.

"Some things are not what they seem."

"That's for sure," Carly grumbled, remembering the way Luke had looked at her the night before. So softly, so sincerely.

"Carly," Aunt Jean said in a flat tone that said, *be reasonable.*

She didn't want to be reasonable. She wanted to be mad. Furious. At Luke and at herself.

Aunt Jean let a long, awkward pause settle in, putting the onus on Carly to speak.

"He's just like my father," Carly said, finally giving in.

Her father had deceived one woman after another, leading each on before dumping her for someone else. Refusing to settle down — ever.

"He's nothing like your father. And you're nothing like your mother," Aunt Jean said.

Carly wiggled her jaw from side to side. She sure hoped she was nothing like her mother. But what if she made the same mistakes?

"Your father needed a strong woman. He never found her," Aunt Jean said sadly.

Carly kicked the ground.

"And you..." Aunt Jean started, then trailed off.

Carly looked up sharply. *Me, what?*

"Did you ever consider how much you're like your father?" Aunt Jean said with no sharpness in her voice whatsoever. "In all the good ways — and the bad."

What was that supposed to mean?

"You're just as stubborn and just as strong," Jean went on. "People look up to you. They follow your lead..."

Carly studied her toes. They did, but she'd never really stepped up to take any responsibility, had she?

"You've broken more than one heart in your time..."

Carly's jaw swung open as she stared at Aunt Jean. "I have not—"

"No?" Jean said so quietly, Carly had to pause and think.

So she'd played around with a lot of men. That didn't mean she'd taken them seriously or led them on.

But... But... She wanted to protest as a whole parade of ex-lovers filed through her mind, their shoulders drooping, their faces drawn.

Shit. She'd always seen those hurried good-byes from her own point of view. She'd never stopped to consider theirs.

"I have the feeling you're like your father in another way, too," Aunt Jean said.

Carly crossed her arms but couldn't resist the bait. "How?"

"He does perfectly well on his own, but he'd be better with a mate. Someone to even him out."

"Maybe I don't want to be evened out. Especially not with a lying son of a—"

Jean's strict look cut her off there. "What did you see?"

Carly rolled her eyes. "More than I needed to."

"What did you see?" Aunt Jean repeated in her stern, teacher voice.

"I saw Audrey leaving the guest house, half dressed."

Jean sighed. "Sweetie, when is Audrey ever properly dressed?"

Carly made a face. Okay, Jean had a point there. Audrey's man-eater dressing habits rarely left much to the imagination. But that wasn't the point. The point was that Luke had run out with Audrey when both were barely dressed. She'd seen Luke. . .

Her thoughts slowed down there. She'd seen Luke, looking like he'd just had a near-miss with a truck. A truck named Audrey, who had a knack for finagling her way into men's beds.

"What exactly did you see?" Jean whispered.

Carly chewed her lip. She'd seen Luke's eyes light up when they met her own, as if his day had only truly started then. She'd practically seen his inner wolf sit up and wag its tail, trying to make a good impression. She'd seen. . .

Crap. She'd seen the hurt in his eyes when she'd rejected him.

A hawk cried in the early morning silence, and a jackrabbit scurried past, dodging prickly pears. The last whiff of night-scented flower wafted through the air. A horse nickered in the distance, and Carly's head jerked up.

"I need to clear my head. . ." she mumbled, heading uphill again. A good, hard ride on a half-wild mustang, that's what she needed.

"Carly," Aunt Jean called.

This time, Carly didn't stop. She stomped right up the hill to the stables, grabbed a bridle and a handful of oats, and headed for the farthest paddock on the right. The one where a black horse kicked and snorted, daring anyone to come close.

"Come on, Diablo," she called, showing him the oats. "You know you want this."

Her voice still had an edge to it, though, and the stallion shied away.

"Come on, baby," she murmured, showing him the oats. Vowing that if the horse didn't come over in the next two minutes, she'd gallop off into the hills on her own two feet.

Maybe on four, because shifting into wolf form had a certain appeal, too.

Scratch that, she decided. Her wolf was just as likely to chase after Luke as to head to the hills, and there was no way she was doing that.

"Come on, Diablo..."

Finally, it worked. She slipped the bridle over the black stallion's head as he mopped up the oats in her hand. When she opened the gate and led him out, his ears immediately perked.

Yeah, she knew that feeling. The need to escape. For freedom — real freedom. From her family, from commitments... even from herself.

With one quick jump, she mounted the stallion's bare back and touched his flanks with her heels. He shot off like a rocket, and she immediately squealed.

"Yes!"

The excitement — the thrill — drew her in, like it always did. Her own personal drug against loneliness and regret.

You promised no regrets, her wolf whispered inside.

She leaned low over Diablo's neck, trying not to think about it. She'd seen the look on Cody's face. Her brothers had probably already booted Luke off the ranch by now. Good-bye and good riddance, right?

The coarse hairs of Diablo's mane whipped her face as her own hair streamed out behind her. She squeezed her knees as the horse thundered over the uneven terrain, heading for the hills. She gave him his head, not caring where he took her as long as it was away.

She ducked a low-hanging branch and hung on when Diablo skittered sideways at the sight of a snake slithering into the bushes.

"Hup," she urged him on. "Hup."

Her mother would have a heart attack, seeing her on that barely tamed mustang, but Carly just grinned into the wind. Even if she fell, she'd heal. She was a shifter, after all.

Shifter healing won't fix a broken heart, her wolf cried inside.

She banished the thought — all thought — and concentrated on the thrill, the high she got from living this close to the edge.

She and Diablo were both panting by the time they reached the midpoint of the mesa, where the winding trail stopped on a wide step in the slope. On one side, a sheer cliff fell away to the valley below, and on the other, the mesa sloped sharply upward. Diablo paused at a cliff's edge, his flanks heaving, nostrils flaring. She patted his shoulder and looked out over the view.

Twin Moon Ranch. Home, but not home.

She shook her head, considering. Maybe she could find another pack to join. Someplace like this, but a little different. Someplace she could get a fresh start on her own terms. Without her mother. Without that ass, Craig. And without that other ass, Luke.

How about North Ridge? Her wolf wagged its tail.

She loved Colorado, and her father had always encouraged her to help him with that pack, but if Luke was headed there. . . no way.

She scanned the vast landscape. Somewhere out there had to be a place for her.

"Nice view, eh?" an edgy voice murmured from behind.

She whipped her head around exactly at the same moment that Diablo reared and spun.

"Whoa," she yelped, grabbing at the horse's mane.

Too late. She was already sliding backward, headed for an ignoble dismount over his tail. She landed on her feet — barely — and stumbled.

Diablo whinnied furiously, flashed his hooves at whoever it was that had spooked them, and thundered away.

"Diablo!" she yelled, running after him.

Three steps later, she pulled up and stiffened at the laughter coming from behind her. She whirled, clenching her fists. Who the hell had the nerve to—

She froze and her jaw dropped. "Craig?"

What the hell was Craig doing here?

"Miss me?" He grinned.

"No," she shot back. She hadn't missed that cocky grin, those greedy, arrogant eyes, or the overwhelming smell of hair gel. She hadn't missed the egotistical bastard one bit.

"What the hell are you doing on pack property?" she demanded, silently counting the men behind him. Five…six…seven.

Craig made a show of looking around, unimpressed. "Oh, is this pack property? So sorry. Someone must have left a gate open."

She frowned. No one ever left gates open at Twin Moon Ranch. And the patrols were usually fastidious about keeping outsiders away.

But, shit. Ty had sent some of their best guards to Colorado to assist her father in case rogues threatened a violent takeover.

She squinted at the other men. Wait a minute. Had Craig banded together with rogues?

One man leered openly. Another looked her slowly up and down. A third whispered something to the man at his side, who grinned. That one was missing a tooth, and the others wore worn, dusty jeans. A few, though, were slicker and more polished, like Craig. Which meant Craig had taken his handful of supporters and formed an alliance with a gang of rogues. Why?

"You're keeping good company these days," she sneered.

Craig waved his hand, unconcerned. "Gotta be flexible when you've got big plans."

"Big plans?"

His grin became a scowl. "Sure. A man's gotta move up in the world. Gotta find my own pack. I had a good lead, too, on a pack in Colorado."

North Ridge. She knew it from the shine in Craig's eyes.

"But surprise, surprise. Someone tipped off that pack that we were coming, so I couldn't execute my plan."

"A plan to take over the pack my father runs?"

He shrugged. "You were the one who messed up Plan A."

Plan A, she realized, was for her to mate to Craig, making him a shoo-in as future alpha of Arroyo Hills or North Ridge pack. An alpha she knew would be no better than Greer, who had only ruled for his own gain.

"And you, apparently, fucked up Plan B," she shot back.

Craig scowled. "Wanna guess what Plan C is?"

She put her hands on her hips. "Slink off into the sunset like your sorry ass deserves?"

A distant rattle sounded from the valley below, and voices carried on the wind, too far to be distinct but audible all the same.

She looked down and saw a wagon and a couple of pack horses that could have passed for a scene from pioneer days. But those were no pioneers. Those were the kids of Twin Moon Ranch.

"Plan C," Craig murmured, nodding at the view.

Carly's blood ran cold.

"You wouldn't," she hissed, picturing Craig and the rogues swooping down on the kids. By the time help arrived…

"Now, why wouldn't I?" Craig scowled. "This pack ruined my plans." He looked right at her. "You ruined my plans. Of course…" He trailed off and grinned, raising his eyebrows at her.

The seven rogues around them stepped closer, boxing her in.

"Of course, what?" she spat, trying to reach Stef or Heather in her mind.

Stef! Heather! Get the kids back to the ranch! Call for help!

Both those women were tough warriors in their own right, but they couldn't possibly defend so many kids from a gang like this.

The problem was, her connection to Stef and Heather wasn't as strong as it was to her siblings, and their minds seemed so busy with the kids, they were deaf to her screams.

"Of course, you could save me all that trouble — and save them." Craig wore the look of a cat who'd just gorged itself on a songbird. A cat with bloody feathers around its mouth.

His ragtag gang of supporters crept forward another inch, but Carly refused to step back. She didn't have room, for one thing. She was mad as hell, for another.

"Save them from you?" she sneered. "Innocent children who've done you no wrong?"

Craig went on as if she hadn't spoken. "Just come with me, baby. No one gets hurt. Not the kids, not you."

She could see the lie in his eyes. She could smell it in his scent.

"I'd treat you well, baby. Just like I promised I would," Craig said.

The shine in his eyes was dark, dangerous. On the outside, he was a charming son from a good family who was eager to move up in the world. On the inside, he harbored a devil who'd stop at nothing until he had what he wanted — leadership of a pack.

Craig couldn't hope to take over Twin Moon pack. But if she acquiesced and went with him, she'd be his entry ticket to North Ridge.

She could see it already: his men pinning her down while Craig ravaged her and delivered the mating bite. Even a forced bite would bind her to that despicable man. It wouldn't matter if she ran away — he'd be able to track her down. And anyway, she doubted he'd let her out of his sight. As for infiltrating North Ridge, all he'd have to do was drug her or beat her up before bringing her to her father and act as her rescuer. Who knew what the man was capable of?

Carly looked around, hoping Diablo would come galloping back. She could hop on and race away in time to warn the kids.

But no Diablo. Nothing but a grinning Craig, who knew right where he had her.

"You and me, baby. We'd be in charge of our own pack," he went on. "We could do anything we want with it."

She held back the words on the tip of her tongue. *You'd be in charge. I would be a slave.*

She flexed her fingers, ready to fight. She could take Craig on. Well, an outside chance, at least, especially if she were fighting for her life. But she certainly wouldn't get far as one against eight.

She cast around for another idea. She could climb down the cliff behind her, but it would take a minute to lower herself over the lip. And once she was on the vertical face, what then? Craig could hurl rocks at her and cast her to certain death or simply keep her pinned there while sending his men to attack the kids.

"Just come with me, baby. Nothing has to happen to those kids."

He pointed. The wagon in the distance creaked to a stop, and the kids came bounding out, milling around like so many cheery hummingbirds.

"You're a monster, you know that?" she sneered.

Craig just grinned and stroked his chin. His freshly shaved chin. "Call it ambition."

She barely heard the words, because something about his close shave struck her. His recently trimmed hair, too. Craig had always spent a little too much time looking in the mirror, but now...

She narrowed her eyes on the men behind Craig — the scrappier, biker types. They were freshly shaved, too. What kind of gang cleaned up before launching an ambush? And how did they even know the kids would be out on a field trip?

She sniffed deeply and caught a whiff of a familiar perfume.

Audrey? her inner wolf roared.

She could picture it perfectly — the rogues sniffing around the town where Audrey ran her salon. She could picture Craig strutting in and turning on his charm to loosen Audrey's tongue.

How's life, sweetheart? Craig had probably asked, warming Audrey up while she treated him to one of her full-frontal shaves.

Audrey would sigh and thrust her boobs even closer to his face. *Life can be lonely on a ranch. Everyone mated but me. And the kids can be such pests. It's impossible to get any peace.*

Craig would have jumped on the chance at information on the pack's most vulnerable members and wheedled the rest out of Audrey, who would have been too busy pole-dancing the man's leg to think about what she was saying.

"You snake," Carly spat, giving Craig the evil eye.

He leaned closer, making her step back. "Maybe all I need is a good woman to tame me. All powerful alphas do."

His voice was so cocky, so full of himself, she nearly slapped him.

I'll tame you, all right, her wolf hissed.

The prospect of shifting to wolf form and letting her claws rip was so, so tempting. But the rogues would shift, too, and they'd be even less predictable when their animal sides took control. Her only real option was to go with Craig, and she knew it. To distract him and try to make a break for it somewhere along the way.

"There's a hard way, and there's an easy way." Craig gestured down the dirt maintenance road that led to the overlook they stood upon.

The front bumper of a truck showed from around a corner with two motorcycles beside it. The vehicles were parked at the foot of the next upward sweep of the mesa, a sheer vertical wall, which sparked a whole new option in her mind. If she ran ahead of Craig, she could climb that, and—

An engine groaned from around the corner, and her hopes fell. Did Craig have more backup coming in?

But Craig's brow furrowed and he spun around, his ears twitching at the sound.

"Who the hell is that?" he barked as a beat-up blue pickup swung into view.

The sun glinted off the windshield, hiding the occupants. Carly held her breath. The driver parked, considered for a long, agonizing minute, then slid slowly out of the cab and stretched to full height.

He was big. Bristly. Clearly not amused.

Luke! Luke! Her inner wolf wagged its tail furiously.

Chapter Fifteen

Luke tore his gaze away from Carly — bold, beautiful Carly. Even surrounded by a gang of rogues, she didn't look the slightest bit afraid.

His wolf grinned in pride. *When is my mate afraid of anything?*

Part of his soul sighed. Carly was likely to charge straight into trouble just to get a closer look. But he doubted that was the case now, judging by the way her fingers flexed like claws.

He wrestled his attention over to the big guy cornering her. The asshole crowding his mate.

The one I'm about to kill? his wolf growled.

Luke took a few steps to the right, trying to pull the rogues' attention away from Carly. If he could draw them over slightly, Carly could make a run for it down the road.

She fixed him with a haughty look that said, *As if I'd run from a fight.*

"Who the hell are you?" the big, clean-cut guy asked.

Luke looked over every member of the gang before answering. He'd never seen the leader before, but right behind him were Steen van Kleij and a couple of his followers. Guys he'd crossed paths with in his wildest, darkest days. The worst kind of bad-hearted rogues who had no business in a place as nice as this. Eight men in total.

"Now look who's here," Steen sneered. "A blast from the past."

Luke inhaled slowly, telling himself not to get riled up.

The kids, Carly's voice hissed in his mind. *We have to keep these assholes away from the kids.*

Luke's eyes darted to the plains far, far below. The second he spotted the kids, his blood ran cold. Ty Hawthorne had sent a contingent of his best men to Colorado as backup in the event of a rogue attack on North Ridge. Evidently, the rogues had given up on that goal but had focused on another — revenge on Twin Moon pack for foiling their plan. A hit-and-run attack of the most cowardly kind.

"Out. Get out." Luke jerked a thumb over his shoulder, planted his feet wide, and crossed his arms

"Yeah. Get the hell out, Craig," Carly said.

Luke glanced at her. *You know this jerk?*

I wish I didn't, she shot back.

Craig laughed and addressed Luke as if Carly weren't even there. "Yeah, I can see why you've been hanging around this ranch. Smells like they have some good pickings here."

Luke tensed.

Craig nodded to himself. "We've been scoping them out, haven't we, boys? That Audrey sure knows how to take care of a man."

Luke ground his teeth and shifted a step farther, edging around the group, hoping Carly would seize the chance to run.

"Which one are you after?" Craig asked, talking about women like so many hunks of beef. "The tall one? That feisty brunette? Such a sweet thing. Though I do prefer blondes, myself."

Luke managed to keep his eyes off Carly, but he couldn't stop the twitch in his jaw. Just a little twitch, but Craig caught it. He looked between Luke and Carly, sniffing deeply. A moment later, his demeanor went from cocky to outraged.

"Bitch." He turned to Carly. "Have you been sleeping around behind my back?"

Luke clenched his fists so hard his nails sliced into his palms. He'd never been so close to jumping into a mindless attack, but he had to stay in control if he was going to win this fight.

Craig spun back at him, sputtering. "You've been sleeping with my woman?"

"She's not yours."

Craig sneered. "And what makes her yours?"

"She's not mine," Luke shot back. It hurt to say it, but it was true. "She's her own person." Luke pinched his lips together and looked at Carly, who was staring at him.

He let out a heavy breath. No matter how much he wanted Carly, she wasn't his and never would be. She'd made that perfectly clear when she stomped away.

Craig advanced, practically snarling. "After we've taken care of you, I'll take care of her. I guarantee I'll take very good care of her."

Luke's blood boiled, and he rolled his shoulders, preparing to shift to wolf form and tear the bastard's throat out. But the rogues spread out — all eight of them — making his mind spin. How the hell were he and Carly going to overcome those odds?

"Like I need to be taken care of," Carly scoffed.

Then another voice called out, and everyone whipped around.

"Hey! What's going on?"

For a heartbeat, Luke's hopes lifted. He could use some backup for sure. But, man. It was Kyle stomping up the road, leading a fidgety black horse wearing a bridle but no saddle. Kyle, who hated him to the bone, no matter how hard he tried to prove himself.

"You okay, Carly?" Kyle's eyes shifted to the rogues. When they skipped to Luke, they retained the same hard look, as if Luke was one of them.

Luke gritted his teeth. When would Kyle understand that he meant no harm? That he was one of the good guys?

When hell froze over, he guessed.

"I'm fine," Carly grunted.

"I got this, man," Luke said, pointing down at the plains. "You take care of that."

Kyle followed his gesture with a cutting look that turned to one of horror the second he recognized the danger the kids were in. His son as well as his mate.

I said, I got this, Luke said, gathering all his willpower to force the words into Kyle's mind.

No, he was nowhere near as confident as he sounded. But if Kyle could help Carly get away, it hardly mattered what happened to him. Kyle and Carly could rush back to the ranch and raise the alarm while Luke held off the rogues as long as he could.

How long do you reckon that might be? the dark voice of doubt murmured in his mind.

A dozen possible outcomes flashed through his mind, and they all ended with him dying under the onslaught of so many rogues.

Are you really ready to risk your ass for a pack that's just cast you out?

Luke thought about it a second. Yes. Yes, he was. Twin Moon might not be his pack, but it was a worthy cause. Worthy enough to risk everything for.

I can hold them off. Go, he urged Kyle. *Take Carly. Protect your family.*

Kyle looked at him with a startled expression, then tilted his head.

Why should I trust you?

Luke scowled. *You don't have to trust me. Just get Carly out of here and raise the alarm. Go!*

Kyle glared at him, then the rogues.

Luke wanted to shake him and yell. *No, I am not plotting anything behind your back. Yes, I have enough honor to do the right thing. Just go, already!*

Sweat broke out over Kyle's brow, and Luke could see him warring with himself. Clearly, Kyle was used to being the honorable one, but his family was in danger.

Just go! another voice insisted — Carly's.

No way, Luke told her. *No way do you stay.*

No way do I go, she barked.

Come on, Carly, Kyle pleaded.

She planted her feet in a clear signal. *You go. Luke and I will hold them off.*

Luke's inner wolf grinned. *"Luke and I." I like the sound of that.*

Yeah, he did, too.

Kyle gave him one last, hard look, then sprang onto Diablo's back and thundered away.

"Shit! Stop him!" Steen yelled. "He'll warn the others."

"Let him warn them," Craig scowled. "I have what I want." His greedy eyes landed on Carly.

"Like hell you do." Carly stepped forward, her eyes aflame.

"Carly, wait—" Luke shouted, suddenly aware of what she was about to do.

Stop me, her eyes screamed. She rolled her shoulders, hunched, and shifted.

For a second, Luke was breathless. Immobile. Craig and the others were too, and thank goodness for that. In one quick flash, Carly went from lithe, confident woman to raging wolf. Her back hunched. Her shirt split down her back, and gloriously smooth skin showed briefly before fur broke out all over it. Fur the same golden hue as her hair. She shook her body once, taking his breath away.

Are you with me or not, Hot Stuff? she growled as she launched herself at Craig.

Luke shook himself out of his stupor and stepped forward.

Hell, yes.

His wolf ripped right out of him, taking over from one stuttering heartbeat to the next. His canines tore through his gums, extending as he turned to take out the nearest rogue, and his jaw narrowed painfully into wolf shape.

Nowhere near the pain these assholes are going to feel, his wolf murmured as all hell broke loose.

Carly knocked Craig over, but the intruder managed to roll clear. Two of his followers shifted and pounced on Carly, but they were too slow. She leaped backward, snarling wildly.

Luke barely tasted the blood of the first rogue he killed, nor that of the second. His pulse hammered as he struck out at one opponent after another, trying to work his way closer to Carly.

"Kill him!" Craig yelled, rallying his men. "But don't hurt the woman. She's mine."

A second later, Craig shifted into wolf form. Carly snarled. Luke roared, swiping at the nearest rogue. No way was he letting anyone drag Carly away. No way.

Adrenaline carried him through the next minute, giving him a high. But the enemy fought back in twos and threes. Steadily, the rogues — lean, mean wolves hardened by a lifetime of fighting — regained the upper hand, pushing him and Carly closer and closer to the cliff's edge.

He gritted his teeth and fought on. For Carly. For the kids. The longer he kept the intruders busy, the longer Kyle had to get the kids to safety.

Steen darted forward. Luke slashed at the rogue's muzzle with his claws and immediately turned to repel the next attacker. It barreled at him with its nose low, protecting its throat. Luke feinted left, then shoved the beast right. The wolf's momentum carried it toward the cliff's edge, and it scrambled desperately for some hold before tumbling out of sight.

The wolf screamed as it fell, reminding Luke just how long that drop was. How lethal.

Carly grunted. *Three down, five to go.*

The other wolves paused momentarily, staring at the spot where their comrade had fallen. Luke half expected a thump when it smashed into the ground, but there was nothing. Just a deathly silence and the eerie whistle of the wind.

Luke peeked over a shoulder at the kids. It was hard to tell through the sweat in his eyes, but the kids appeared to have clustered around the wagon again. Had they been warned? Was help on its way?

With a snarl, Carly jumped into a counterattack, and Luke snapped his focus back to the fight.

Craig let out a bellow, and the other wolves growled, pushing forward as one. Two of them slammed into Luke at the same time, gaining precious ground. The earth crumbled under Luke's rear foot, and for one terrifying moment, he clawed at thin air. It wasn't terrifying in the sense of his own death — just knowing that if he fell, Carly would be on her own. She could fight like a banshee, but even she couldn't beat so many rogues on her own.

Carly butted one of the two rogues, giving Luke enough time to get all four paws earthbound again. But crap, had it been close. His pulse raced in a staccato beat, and he let out a roar that echoed off the hill behind them.

Will not let my mate down, he howled, powering forward again. He slashed at the side of the wolf facing Carly, then shoved it off the cliff.

Get them, Craig bellowed.

Luke grinned at the frustration in his foe's voice. He and Carly were doing a damn good job holding back the remaining wolves, but how long could they hold out?

Long enough, his wolf promised. *As long as it takes.*

Every second bought Carly an extra chance. Kyle would rush to the kids first, but he'd get word to Carly's family, and they'd come racing for her.

As long as it takes, Luke promised himself.

But the wounds he'd sustained sent red flares of alarm through his body. His right shoulder had been torn open, making him feel lopsided. One ear had been sliced lengthwise by the enemy's fangs, and blood trickled over his snout, stinging his eyes.

Every second counts, he told himself, squinting into the midday light.

A rangy wolf with a dark coat — Steen — darted forward, making for his injured shoulder. Luke sidestepped and snapped just as a scuffle broke out behind him.

No! Carly yelped as three more rogues pushed forward in a coordinated attack.

A two-pronged attack, he realized, with Steen coming his way and three headed for Carly.

Everything became a blur of sound and motion. The ivory of his attackers' fangs stained crimson with blood. The flash of fur in shades of brown and gray. Carly's grunts of defiance as the rogues mobbed her. The crush of pebbles and dry earth under his paws. The void of the cliff's face just inches to his right.

Steen was bigger but a little too slow, and Luke managed to sidestep his attacks. But the bastard formed a wall between him and Carly, making it impossible to see how she was faring.

Steen reared up and tackled him, and they wrestled perilously close to the cliff's edge. Luke's shoulder throbbed, but he kept all his focus on the enemy, looking for an opening until finally — there! — the wolf's neck flashed, unprotected for a split second.

Luke opened his jaws and snapped, locking the rogue in a death hold. The acrid taste of blood flooded his mouth, and the wolf moaned, then slowly went limp.

Get off me! Carly's wolf cries said. *No! No!*

Luke held his enemy until the life bled right out of him, then released Steen and spun around, snarling so hard his throat hurt.

Luke! Carly screamed.

Mine! Craig howled, helping the two rogues who'd overpowered her. They dragged her forward by the paw as she wrestled and lashed out with her free limbs.

Not yours! Luke growled, barreling forward. In his mind, the real-life image of Craig merged with an ugly image from his memory — Greer, the ruthless alpha of North Ridge pack. Greer, coming to claim whatever he deemed his.

Get him, Luke urged his wolf. *Let Greer feel our revenge.*

He'd once met an old coyote shifter who'd had a theory that all evil was connected. That an attack on one manifestation of evil could make itself felt on all evil.

Luke pushed forward, hoping to hell that was true. Because he was about to rip Craig to pieces, and he wanted Greer to feel that pain all the way from his grave.

You die, he roared, launching himself at Craig.

They slammed together a second later, then broke apart, both reeling from the impact.

Luke! Carly cried as one of her attackers bit deeper into her leg.

Luke blinked the stars out of his eyes just in time to see Craig leap at him. On a good day, Luke would have pivoted at the last second then whipped around to grab Craig by the neck. But Craig had been staying at the periphery of the fight, saving his strength, while Luke had been fighting for dear life. Was his timing sharp enough to pull off that move?

Concentrate! his human side yelled at his wolf. *Get Greer!*

The thought caught in his mind. Was that Greer or Craig?

Whatever, his wolf snarled, shifting its haunches for the move he had to get exactly right.

Craig came at him with jaws gaping wide, but Luke kept his focus on the wolf's shoulders. The angle, the distance, the speed—

Now! he urged his wolf.

His rear leg nearly gave out on him, but he darted aside then twisted and buried his teeth in the side of Craig's neck. Craig howled in pain and rolled, crushing Luke, who refused to let go.

Craig is Greer. Greer is Craig, his wolf chanted, releasing his jaws just long enough to work his way closer to his foe's neck. He clamped down hard, and Craig twisted under him.

Kill him. Kill him, he told himself, feeling the blood flow.

Craig choked and kicked.

Mercy... Mercy...

Luke snarled. Had Craig ever shown anyone mercy? Had Greer?

This is for Carly. For my sister. For every victim Greer ever claimed, he told himself, giving a mighty shake until he heard Craig's neck snap.

Luke nearly flopped to the ground, but he dragged himself up to help Carly. Two wolves remained, and they were hustling her away.

No, they won't, his wolf growled, attacking the one with its jaws clamped around her leg.

The rogue howled and released Carly, who immediately rolled to her feet. Luke used his remaining strength to bulldoze the nearest wolf over the edge and into oblivion, while Carly fought in a series of lightning-fast bites and slashes.

But damn. They were fighting on the edge of the cliff now. The sheer, crumbling edge.

Luke saw it all in slow motion as he turned to help. The wide whites of the last rogue's eyes. The flaying motion of its front legs that swept Carly sideways, toward the precipice.

The rogue reached forward as its rear legs went over the cliff. It clamped its jaws over Carly's rear leg in a last-ditch effort that said, *If I die, you die.*

Carly scrambled to get free, but the wolf was too big, and Luke's exhausted wolf was a tick too slow. The rogue disappeared over the edge, dragging Carly with it.

No! Luke howled, stretching forward. *No!*

Luke! Carly's eyes went wide as her paws scratched helplessly at the loose soil.

Chapter Sixteen

The world tipped sideways, and thin air pulled at Carly's limbs.

If I die, you die, the rogue clamped to her leg snarled as he dragged her over the edge.

She wanted to turn and spit at him. *You're the only one who's going to die, asshole.*

She gathered all her energy for a mighty kick the way she'd seen Luke summon the last of his energy to fight Craig. Luke, who'd fought with the strength of ten wolves, exactly the way her brothers had fought for their mates.

Mate, her wolf whispered. *Mate.*

She took a deep breath and kicked with her free leg, dislodging the rogue. He screamed and clawed at thin air as he fell. And fell and fell and—

The rogue's cry was cut short by a heavy thump.

Carly yelped, finding herself sliding after him. The wind whistled beneath her, pulling at her legs.

The world decelerated into super slow motion, and all sound faded away as she observed her own doom in a surprisingly detached way. Her wolf claws raked parallel lines into the earth, unable to find a grip. Luke's eyes went wide, and his lips moved as he lunged for her.

Shift, his voice boomed into her mind. *Shift!*

He seemed so panicked. So scared. And shit, so was she.

Because you're about to die, you idiot, her wolf screamed.

Which was strange, because she'd brushed shoulders with death before. Why was this different? Why was she so scared this time?

Because you have so much to lose now, her wolf cried as her fate unfolded, one agonizing millisecond at a time.

Another inch of her body slipped over the edge, tipping her center of gravity as her mind spun with a dozen *I'm-not-ready-to-die* thoughts she'd never had before.

My mate. My future. My life, her wolf mourned.

Luke's eyes flashed, and she saw the same regrets there. The heart-to-heart talk they'd never had the courage to have. The hand-in-hand walks, living life at a slower, stop-and-smell-the-roses pace. The challenges they'd never take on together because it all ended right here.

Shift! Luke yelled, reaching for her. *Shift!*

His paw uncurled and became a hand, and his fur receded into a field of skin covered with dirt and blood.

"Shift!"

The words echoed off the hills and in her mind.

She stretched her right leg forward, and it hurt like hell because wolf shoulders didn't hinge that far.

Shift, she cried at her wolf. *Let me shift.*

The beast gave in, letting her human side emerge. She reached farther, crying out at the scrape of dry earth against her bare skin. She aimed for Luke's fingertips, but they seemed so far. Her upper body slid over the edge of the cliff.

Time to free fall, the wind whispered, swirling around her torso. *Come on. It will be a thrill.*

For the first time in her life, she didn't want a thrill.

"Hold on!" Luke yelled, his human voice still scratchy with the sound of his beast.

Their hands slapped together, and his fingers curled around hers in a steely grip.

"Luke," she screamed as gravity yanked her the rest of the way off the ledge. To the void. To the three-hundred-foot drop. To certain death.

Tight as Luke's hand was around hers, she was still falling. Which meant Luke was falling, too. Both of them, going over the edge.

Then Carly lurched. Her shoulder wrenched. Luke grunted.

She looked down, and the distance to the ground wasn't decreasing, because she wasn't falling any more. She was swinging in midair, suspended from above by the man who refused to let go.

"Hang on," Luke said.

She looked up and understood why his voice was so shaky. He was hanging on to a root with one hand while the other clung to her. They both swung in thin air.

When she locked eyes with Luke, the words he'd challenged Craig with echoed through her mind. *She's not yours. She's not mine. She's her own person.*

A worthy mate. A mate who won't rob you of your freedom, her wolf cried. *You see?*

She gulped. Yes. Now she could see. But was it too late? Luke couldn't support the weight of them both with only one hand. Not for long, anyway.

"Swing me closer," she said, reaching around blindly with her feet. "I can grab hold of something."

"Grab hold of what?" His face pinched with the strain.

She cursed inside, because he was right. The cliff fell away in a concave sweep, and no matter what she tried, there was nothing within reach.

"You can't hold us both."

"Watch me," he said through clenched teeth.

His deep, dark eyes swirled with fear and determination. Fear for what might happen to her, not him. And determination for...for...

"No, Luke. Don't," she cried, watching a crazy plan unfold in his eyes.

Her feet were dangling in midair, and his eyes focused on the long, terrible fall behind her. She had an awful vision of both of them tumbling to their deaths, with Luke attempting a stunt like wrapping himself around her body to take the brunt of the fall. She might survive, but he wouldn't.

She could see him calculating it all out, and it scared her to death.

"Don't you dare be my hero," she said fiercely.

He let out a bitter chuckle. "At least I'll be that."

She shook her head. "You said no regrets."

"I meant our night together — not the mess I've made of my life."

The glint in his eye let her know he was keeping her distracted while he calculated what he had to do. How much twist he'd need in midair to be able to grab her around the waist. How he'd clamp his arms and legs around her body and swing around, making sure he'd be the first to hit.

She started playing it out for herself, hoping to find some way to survive, but no matter what she imagined, the fall always ended in a slamming halt and death.

My death, his eyes said. *Not yours.*

"No. No way," she said. There had to be some other way. "What if we—"

She jerked her head up without finishing her sentence. The ground above them had filled with the sound of scuffling feet.

No! her wolf cried, picturing more rogues. Maybe Craig had reinforcements. Maybe some of the rogues they'd thought dead were wounded and limping back to finish her and Luke off. Maybe—

"Holy shit," someone cried, and a wave of blond hair appeared above Luke at the ledge.

"Cody!" she cried. Never had she been so glad to see her brother. Never.

"Christ. Don't let go," Cody barked.

"Never crossed my mind," Luke murmured.

More voices sounded and arms reached down, hauling Luke up — and Carly with him. Luke's body scraped over the ground as the wolves of Twin Moon Ranch manhandled him up.

"We got you, Carly."

"Hang on, sweetheart."

All those words of encouragement were aimed at her, not Luke, and she wanted to scream. She nearly did, too, but something better crossed her mind.

I got you, Luke. She pushed the words into his mind. *Hang on.*

He grinned despite the hell he had to be going through. *I got you, too.*

Someone grabbed her arm and pulled her to safety, but when they tore her away from Luke, she almost cried.

"Oh, my God," someone said.

"Are you all right?"

"Carly, are you okay?"

She ignored all of them and used her last ounce of energy to crawl over to where Luke lay. His chest heaved, and his hands were clenched as if he was still holding her. She half fell, half flung herself at him in an embrace.

"Now wait a minute," Ty protested.

"Carly," Cody warned.

Something in her snapped, and she whirled. "This is my mate, got it? Mine."

"But—" Ty started.

She snarled back, out of patience, out of energy. "He slaved away for our pack. He did everything you asked for and more. He saved the kids, and he saved me. Jesus, what more do you want?"

The landscape seemed to go totally still — just like her packmates.

Ty looked at Cody. Cody looked at the ground. Tina was there, too, staring.

"Your mate, huh?" Tina whispered. To her credit, though, her voice was sincere, not doubtful or teasing.

"My mate," Carly cried, glaring at them all. One by one, her siblings had won their mates. Well, it was her turn now. Who cared if she'd been wrong about how important mates were? Now, she understood. And no one was stopping her. No one.

She must have made it pretty damn clear, because Ty flipped his hands up, giving in.

"Well...all right, then," Cody murmured, backing away with the dawn of a grin.

Tina nodded and motioned to Luke. "All yours, then. Your mate."

The adrenaline spike that had fueled Carly's outburst faded away. She collapsed over Luke, hugging him fiercely.

"My turn to hold you tight," she murmured, burying her face against his neck.

Luke's arms curled around her body, and they lay together, panting as one, ignoring the voices that slowly, carefully piped up again.

"Um, Carly..."

Yes, she was naked after shifting, and so was Luke. Who cared?

"Carly, we really ought to..."

Someone touched her shoulder, and she growled. Let anyone try to get a crowbar between her and Luke. She'd never, ever let go. Never.

"Carly, are you sure you're all right?"

That was Tina, and at first, Carly ignored the light touches on her back. But when she caught the pain in her sister's voice, she softened. There was pain and worry in all those voices surrounding her.

"God, Carly, you nearly fell."

Her brothers and sister were there, worried out of their minds. They were chattering, pleading, checking that she was all right. She could hear their inner wolves whining with emotion — even Ty, who never let any emotion slip out through the chinks in his armor. Never.

Except for right now.

Tears welled up in her eyes. Hot, blinding tears that took her by surprise, because she never cried. Never.

But, crap. She was doing it now.

How much pain had she inflicted on her family all these years? How many thrill-seeking acts had she jumped into without thinking of anyone else? Late nights in iffy bars. Hurtling along on her motorcycle at breakneck speeds. Thousand-foot free-climbs. If her loved ones felt even a fraction of the fear she experienced at the idea of losing Luke, it would be shattering.

The tears became sobs that wracked her body. How would she ever make up what she'd done to them? How could she have been so selfish for so long? How—

Two strong arms circled her and pulled her tight. Luke rocked her gently. Her siblings murmured, assuring her it would be all right. Love poured in from every side, warming her like the sun. Love so real and intense, it hurt, but it felt good at the same time. The way crying felt right now.

She cried until the tears dried up — although not against Luke's neck, which was a sticky mess, not that he seemed to mind. Someone threw a shirt over her, and slowly, she caught her breath.

"You okay?" Luke whispered.

She ran a hand over his shoulder then stroked his cheek. "Yeah. Are you?"

He tightened his hug, and his voice was muffled, but she caught his words, all right. "I am now."

She took a deep breath and pulled away just far enough to speak to the others. "I'm okay. Thanks. I'm okay."

Her wolf wagged its tail weakly, and in her mind, she wound her furry body around Luke's. *We're okay. We're okay.*

We? he asked quietly.

We, she said firmly.

Chapter Seventeen

One week later...

Carly stood at the ranch gate with her arms wrapped around her middle. It was almost time to leave Arizona, and she was still digesting recent events. A fresh breeze ruffled her hair, and the scent of spring was everywhere. Soon, the cacti would come alive with vivid pinkish-purple flowers, and the first of the snapdragons wouldn't be far behind.

Spring. A fresh start. She could feel it right around the corner.

Her own personal spring, too.

She snuggled deeper into Luke's leather jacket and fingered the bite mark on her neck, reliving the best moment of her life — the moment Luke had claimed her as his mate. He'd let her mark him first — the man knew her too well — and *that* had been the best moment of her life until a few minutes later when he reciprocated. They'd just reached the peak of incredibly fiery sex, and the second he sank his teeth into her neck, her world exploded with light. Love. Hope.

"Told you you don't have to speed around on motorcycles to get a real thrill." Tina had said with a wicked grin when Carly shared how good it felt. "And the best thing is, you can do it again and again."

As if Carly hadn't figured that out yet. She and Luke had sequestered themselves away for most of the past week, going at it like bunnies. Making up for a lifetime of loneliness, it felt like. A loneliness she'd always managed to hide from herself until she met him.

Lonely no more, her wolf smiled. *And never again.*

She glanced back at the guest house where Luke waited in the shade of the porch. He knew she needed a few moments alone before leaving the ranch. He'd even said as much the day after the fight.

I don't have to crowd you to love you.

But he was there for her, as he'd been when she needed him most.

I always will be, he said, whispering into her mind.

They were that tuned in to each other. That in sync.

Tina wasn't kidding when she'd said, "I told you mating was worth it."

Carly had to agree. That was the crazy thing. Years ago, her mother had fallen head over heels for a man she barely knew — a possessive alpha type, no less — Carly's dad. And Carly had spent her whole life thinking, *Look where that got her.* But now she'd gone and fallen head over heels for a man she barely knew — an alpha type, of all things — and it didn't even hurt. It just felt good.

Really good, her wolf hummed.

"Hey," Luke murmured, slipping his arms around her.

She turned her head to meet his kiss. "Sneaking up on me again, mister?"

He nuzzled her slowly. "You need more time alone?"

She hugged his arms as her wolf answered. *No, thanks. I've had quite enough time alone.*

"Want to take a little walk?"

She nodded, and they set off slowly, because life didn't feel like it had to be lived in a rush any more. On the contrary, she wanted to slow down and savor every moment with her man.

She and Luke walked down the open square in the center of the ranch then turned left past the supply shed. All the childhood stories she'd been tempted to share had come tumbling out over the past week — including the one about how she'd crawled after a skunk when she was five — and they'd laughed and laughed. Luke shared his stories, too — funny stories from a long time ago. Warm memories of his childhood, and yes, bad memories, too. It hurt just to hear what he'd been through, but part of the invisible burden on his shoulders seemed to ease after that.

The chip on her shoulder did, too.

"Can you make it from this one to that one?" Luke asked, detouring to the tree stumps Carly used to jump between as a kid.

She perched on one while he stepped up on another, and they hopped along the two parallel lines. When they jumped off at the other end, they both wore ear-to-ear grins.

"Aunty Carly! Aunty Carly!"

"Uncle Luke! Uncle Luke!"

Two kids ran up, bright, happy, and blissfully free of all the baggage of adults. The whole pack had accepted Luke after that day up on the cliffs, even if it would take time for the underlying tension to dissipate. The kids, on the other hand, accepted him as if he'd been family all along.

"Aunty Carly, do you really have to leave today?" Holly asked.

"Yes, sweetie."

"Can I come visit you and Grandpa at North Ridge?" Tana asked.

Carly exchanged glances with Luke. Her father had been surprisingly positive when she'd called to say she wanted to move to North Ridge with Luke.

"I'm not getting any younger," her father had grumbled. "Just tell that whippersnapper he's got to work his way up the ranks like everyone else."

That, she knew Luke could handle. No problem.

"Of course. You can visit any time," Carly said.

"Are you going to be the new alpha there?" Tana asked Luke.

"Well... I guess we'll see," he said, looping an arm over Carly's shoulders.

Carly snorted. It was just a matter of time, she knew. Yes, Luke would have to work his way up the ranks as her father had said, but given how he'd won over the wolves of Twin Moon Ranch, Luke would be leading North Ridge pack in no time. Her father was a strong alpha, but he was a grouchy old coot, too, and she'd bet anything the pack was ready for a powerful young alpha like Luke — the kind who actually knew how to smile from time to time.

"You could be like Mommy," Tana said to her. "Daddy says he's in charge of the ranch, and Mommy's in charge of him."

Carly hid her own grin. Yeah, she had a few ideas about her own role at North Ridge. But she'd have to work her way up, just like Luke.

"I want to be alpha someday," Tana said earnestly.

Luke tousled her hair. "I bet you will be. I bet you will be."

Carly had been looking forward to a quiet, good-bye walk across the ranch with Luke, but walking with the girls was fun, too. Luke seemed to enjoy it as much as she did, joking with the kids and admiring all the things they pointed out.

"Oh! See the pretty butterfly?" Holly cried out.

"That's my favorite pony over there," Tana said.

"And look at this rock!" Holly exclaimed, handing Luke a pebble. "Isn't it nice?"

Carly glanced at Luke and knew he was thinking the same thing — that the next generation at North Ridge could grow up in an era of peace and wonder like the kids of Twin Moon Ranch. That fear and suffering at the hands of a corrupt alpha were a permanent part of the past.

He squeezed her hand and smiled at the kids. "That's a great rock, Holly."

"You can keep it."

"I can keep it? Wow. Thanks." He slipped it in his pocket.

The man was good with kids. Carly looked at him out of the corner of her eye.

Just don't get any crazy ideas, she told him.

What ideas? he replied far too innocently.

Don't go thinking I'll be having kids or anything. Just because I mated doesn't mean my life has to end.

Maybe not having kids soon, her wolf murmured. *But someday. . .*

Yeah, she liked the idea of someday. A lot. Not that she'd admit as much. . . yet.

Kids? Luke said. *Nah. Not sure I'd make a good father.*

She stopped abruptly, tugged on his hand, and whispered, "Someday, I'll prove you wrong."

His eyebrows shot up. "Promise?"

She nodded firmly, liking the idea more and more. "Promise."

"What do you promise?" Tana asked.

"Um. . . that you and Holly can visit us in North Ridge soon."

"Hooray!" Tana cried.

"Hooray!" Holly echoed. "Can Mommy and Daddy come, too?"

Carly laughed, but Luke laughed even harder, and the sound echoed off the hills.

"Any of you can come any time. You're all invited." He pointed down at the ranch. "But right now, I think it's time for us to get going."

As they finished the loop, Carly soaked in the views. The patchwork of yards and houses in the central part of the ranch below. The pastures that spread all around, fading gradually into the scrub of the desert. The rocky mesas and the winding dirt road to the highway and the outside world. Home?

Home is where the heart is, Aunt Jean always said.

Carly turned and hugged Luke, murmuring one word. "Home."

The hug turned into a kiss and the kiss nearly heated her up all over again, but Holly and Tana giggled, reminding her where she was and why.

She cleared her throat and broke away from Luke.

More of that later. I promise, she said. *But first things first.*

His eyes were so dark, she still couldn't tell if they were black or brown, but the way they shone, it didn't matter.

"First things first," he agreed, taking her hand.

A little crowd had gathered by the time they reached Luke's truck, ready to say good-bye. Carly hugged everyone a little longer and tighter than she usually did when she left Twin Moon. But when she thought ahead, her heart thumped faster, and part of her wanted to rush out and get started with her new life at North Ridge. Luke still had a few wrongs to right, as well as a pack to lead when the time was right. Carly needed a pack to contribute to, as well — a pack where she wasn't someone's kid sister but her own person. Settling down in Colorado would also strengthen Twin Moon pack by cementing a new alliance with North Ridge.

It's perfect, her wolf hummed, more content than it had ever been.

"Promise you'll visit soon," Tina said as they said their good-byes.

"Say hi to Dad," Cody said. "And don't feel like you have to rush him back here any time soon. We kind of like how peaceful it is."

Carly play-punched her brother in the arm. Yes, their dad could be a real pain in the neck. As the youngest of the Hawthorne siblings, though, she'd always had an easier relationship with him than the others. So, who knew? Maybe her dad would even stay at North Ridge for a while.

"First things first," she murmured, as much to herself as to Cody.

"Bye, Carly," Ty said, gruff as can be — but his hug was a little tighter than usual. And the way he shook hands with Luke made her smile stretch wide.

My mate is something else, her wolf hummed with pride.

That, he was. Luke could fight like the devil, but he'd proven he could humble himself, too. He'd put his life on the line not just for her, but for the entire pack. He'd put his pride on the line, too, and proven himself in every possible way.

"Take care," Heather said.

"Visit soon," Lana added.

Just about every member of the pack was there to say good-bye. Everyone but Audrey, who'd been confronted by Ty and Cody shortly after the rogue attack. Carly had never seen either of her brothers that close to exploding with rage. She would have liked to share a piece of her mind with Audrey, too, but it was too late. Audrey, pale and shaking, had driven away right after the meeting and hadn't been heard from since. Most pack members had breathed a sigh of collective relief.

Which meant Carly's good-byes could be made without bitterness, just heartfelt emotion as she hugged and kissed one person after another.

"Thanks," Ty said to Luke. His voice was low, loading the word with sincerity. "Thanks."

She squeezed Luke's free hand. *Mate. My perfect mate.*

"No," Luke said. "Thank you."

Both men stood there for a while, stuck for words. Still, the trust and gratitude Ty gave Luke through a simple handshake said more than any words could.

Lana winked at her. *Who says communication isn't Ty's thing?*

"Thanks, everyone," Carly said, moving things along.

She and Luke were about to get in that beat-up blue Ford of his when a voice called out.

"Wait."

Everyone turned around, and Carly froze when she saw Kyle hurrying up. Kyle, who had every reason to treat Luke like a mortal enemy.

Carly stiffened, and Luke did, too.

The closer Kyle came, the slower he moved, and he chewed on his bottom lip before grinding to a stop in front of Luke. He dragged a hand through his spiky hair, and with the other, he steadied his son, who was perched on his shoulders.

"Came to say bye," he said, talking to the ground. Slowly, he raised his gaze to Luke's face. "Bye and thanks." He patted his son's foot as he said it, making it clear what he was thankful for.

Luke didn't say anything at first, but his Adam's apple bobbed up and down.

"Like I said," Luke said a moment later, sounding a little raspy, "I came here to thank you."

When he and Kyle shook hands, Carly had to hide the sigh building inside her.

Stef, Kyle's mate, beamed, and when she hugged Luke, Kyle didn't even growl.

"Thank you so much," Stef said. "Thank you."

She looked a lot like the other parents around who hugged their kids tighter and nodded at Luke.

Thank you. Thank you.

Carly could have savored that moment forever, but Luke looked around awkwardly, not quite sure what to do.

"Well, we'd better get going," she said, tugging him toward the vehicle. "Thanks, everyone."

Luke let out a long, relieved breath, climbed into the truck, and started it up.

Everyone waved and called their final good-byes as Luke put the Ford in gear and slowly rolled down the driveway.

"Bye-bye!"

"Have a good trip."

"Visit soon."

"Don't drive too fast!"

Carly stuck her head out the window to blow her sister a kiss. Kyle and Stef were hugging, and Heather had a hand on Cody's shoulder — each woman proud of her man.

Just like Carly, who rested her hand on Luke's thigh.

She looked up as the truck passed under the ranch gateway. The ranch brand swung overhead, as it did every time she arrived or departed. But this time, the metal glinted in the sun, almost like it was winking at her. Or was that destiny?

She settled into her seat and looked forward, ready for her new life.

"Bet he's not sad to see me go," Luke murmured, looking at Kyle in the rearview mirror.

"Nah. Not anymore."

Luke nodded. "True. He's a good man."

She took his hand and kissed it. "Just like you."

Luke cleared his throat sharply, then tried to joke it off. "Think you can live with that?"

"Oh, believe me, I can." She tickled his ear. "Good in all the right ways, with just enough bad to keep things interesting."

He grinned and picked up speed, making the pickup rattle down the dirt road to the highway. Her Triumph was strapped in the back, making a racket. She'd been ready to leave it behind, but Luke insisted she bring it along.

We don't have to give up every part of the past, he'd said. *Besides, you'll need it to take me for a ride from time to time.*

She liked the sound of that. A lot.

"You good?" she asked, catching him glance back.

Luke didn't answer right away, but when he did, he gripped her hand. "First time in years I've left a place and actually felt like I'll miss it. In fact, it's the first time since I left North Ridge as a kid."

She put her hand over his. "Well, then. I guess we're going to the right place."

They both looked north, imagining Colorado, and she could sense his heart swell. Hers did, too.

"We sure are," he murmured. "We sure are, my mate."

Sneak Peek: Damnation

DESERT ROOTS wraps up the Twin Moon series, but your favorite Twin Moon heroes and heroines all make repeat appearances in the BLUE MOON SALOON books, a spin-off series featuring bear and wolf shifters looking for a second chance at life and love. The action, emotion, and passion all kicks off with DAMNATION, Book 1.

DAMNATION

He hasn't forgotten her, and she sure hasn't forgiven him.

Jessica Macks is a she-wolf on the run from a band of murderous rogues. When she finds a job at a shifter bar, it seems like a safe haven from her hunted life on the road. But the minute she walks through the swinging doors of the Blue Moon Saloon and comes face-to-face with the man she once loved, she's tempted to march right back out. No way, no how is she risking her heart to that infuriating alpha bear again.

Simon Voss thought he lost everything in an ambush months before: his home, his family, his past. His new job at the Blue Moon Saloon is a desperately needed fresh start on life. Then along comes Jessica, the irresistible she-wolf his clan forced him to reject years before. When Simon is obliged to hire Jessica and work side by side with the one woman to ever make his bear go wild, he's half in heaven, half in hell. He hasn't forgotten her, and she sure as hell hasn't forgiven him. Is this just another path to heartbreak or his last chance to claim his destined mate?

Behind the doors of the Blue Moon Saloon, alpha shifters confront their darkest fears and their deepest desires. Each book is a complete standalone story — no cliffhangers!

Get your copy of DAMNATION today! Available as ebook,
paperback, and audiobook.

156

Books by Anna Lowe

The Wolves of Twin Moon Ranch

Desert Hunt (the Prequel)

Desert Moon (Book 1)

Desert Blood (Book 2)

Desert Fate (Book 3)

Desert Heart (Book 4)

Desert Rose (Book 5)

Desert Roots (Book 6)

Desert Yule (a short story)

Desert Wolf: Complete Collection (Four short stories)

Sasquatch Surprise (a Twin Moon spin-off story)

Aloha Shifters - Jewels of the Heart

Lure of the Dragon (Book 1)

Lure of the Wolf (Book 2)

Lure of the Bear (Book 3)

Lure of the Tiger (Book 4)

Love of the Dragon (Book 5)

Lure of the Fox (Book 6)

Aloha Shifters - Pearls of Desire

Rebel Dragon (Book 1)

Rebel Bear (Book 2)

Rebel Lion (Book 3)

Rebel Wolf (Book 4)

Rebel Heart (A prequel to Book 5)

Rebel Alpha (Book 5)

Fire Maidens - Billionaires & Bodyguards

Fire Maidens: Paris (Book 1)

Fire Maidens: London (Book 2)

Fire Maidens: Rome (Book 3)

Fire Maidens: Portugal (Book 4)

Fire Maidens: Ireland (Book 5)

Blue Moon Saloon

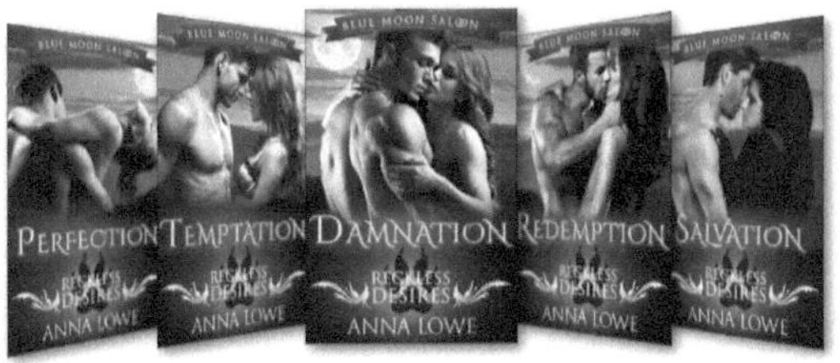

Perfection (a short story prequel)

Damnation (Book 1)

Temptation (Book 2)

Redemption (Book 3)

Salvation (Book 4)

Deception (Book 5)

Celebration (a holiday treat)

Shifters in Vegas

Paranormal romance with a zany twist

Gambling on Trouble

Gambling on Her Dragon

Gambling on Her Bear

Serendipity Adventure Romance

Off the Charts

Uncharted

Entangled

Windswept

Adrift

Travel Romance

Veiled Fantasies

Island Fantasies

visit www.annalowebooks.com

About the Author

USA Today and Amazon bestselling author Anna Lowe loves putting the "hero" back into heroine and letting location ignite a passionate romance. She likes a heroine who is independent, intelligent, and imperfect – a woman who is doing just fine on her own. But give the heroine a good man – not to mention a chance to overcome her own inhibitions – and she'll never turn down the chance for adventure, nor shy away from danger.

Anna loves dogs, sports, and travel – and letting those inspire her fiction. On any given weekend, you might find her hiking in the mountains or hunched over her laptop, working on her latest story. Either way, the day will end with a chunk of dark chocolate and a good read.

Visit AnnaLoweBooks.com

9 781953 468208